FAMILY PLANNING

ACKNOWLEDGEMENTS

I would like to thank my beautiful wife Caroline for her continued support and advice whilst writing Family Planning. Caroline, and my son Andrew continue to be my biggest triumph and greatest pleasure. Thanks also to my amazing work colleagues and football peers, who patiently listened to endless ideas and varied plot developments. A special mention to my editor Lisa McKenzie, and my proofreader Derek Crossan. Your friendly ear and critical eye allowed me to adapt and grow the story into its now published form. Family and friends really are the greatest gift in this life. Respect them, challenge them, support them, love them.

CHAPTER 1

THE DRIVE

Thursday, 26th October 2023.

Frank Smith sat in the driver's seat of his Range Rover Overfinch. The imposing shadow of Edinburgh's iconic Usher Hall loomed to his left. Southbound on Lothian Road was nose-to-tail traffic, an infinity of dipped headlights shone through relentless, bouncing rain. Frank sensed the other drivers' frustration, defined by dozens of short, sharp horn blasts. It seemed no one was getting anywhere fast. Streaming road water comfortably outpaced every queuing vehicle. The start-stop nature of the journey only exaggerated the muscular tone of Frank's purring engine. His huge SUV suggested three things to any inquisitive onlookers: wealth, power and happiness.

Two out of three ain't bad, right?

On the surface, Frank usually presented as a warm, friendly figure of quick wit and composure, yet he clearly carried an air of unpredictability and genuine devilment. Those connected to, or aware of organised crime in the city, knew exactly who Frank was. His reputation had grown exponentially over the years and his name was now legendary. His ominous presences still lingered over many of Edinburgh's broken neighbourhoods, like the pungent and claustrophobic coal smog of the 17th Century. Auld Reekie indeed. Even those more innocent living in and around the city knew his name as a bare minimum and respected what it represented. You either wanted to be affiliated with Frank Smith, or you hoped and prayed you never came across him.

Almost affectionately, Frank was referred to as 'The Cunt's Cunt' in certain business circles, due to his multidimensional personality and innate ability to find pragmatic solutions to varying challenges and predicaments. In years gone by, adversaries and associates alike labelled him as; 'The Nastiest Cunt', 'The Smoothest Cunt' and 'The Smartest Cunt'. As labels were embellished and exaggerated over time, his standing across the city had reached cult status.

Frank squinted at the glaring headlights. Each passing vehicle illuminated his cabin, exposing his bloodshot, teary eyes. He looked manic, almost possessed. He screamed in annoyance, "Bit of fucking rain and suddenly no cunt can drive! Hurry the fuck up!" Both gloved hands trembled as he frenetically gripped the waxy, aniline steering wheel. His right ankle was rigid as he accelerated and decelerated between the changing traffic lights and scattered roadwork signs.

Uncharacteristically, Frank had banged two lines of cocaine before jumping into his executive gas guzzler. He hadn't personally touched ching in almost 15 years, he fucking hated the thought of sniffing the petrol fragranced powder. Frank was very well versed on the risky additives and fillers used to cut cocaine: Fentanyl, Boric acid, Levamisole and Amphetamine, to list just a few. Indeed, he was forever warning Amber about its extreme unpredictability and endless dangers. He'd witnessed first-hand its ability to perforate noses, stop hearts, scramble brains and break families. The half gram he'd stumbled upon was from her designer clutch bag that she'd left on the kitchen table. Normally, such a discovery would result in a flush down the toilet, accompanied by a fiery domestic argument. But, on this occasion he needed a stiffener to settle his own nerves. He'd deal with her later.

Frank had been betrayed in the worst way. He was utterly heartbroken, and was looking to take his incandescent rage out on the perpetrator. He had always stated that any punishment should match the crime, "No point going tits over trivial issues." He'd previously felt that others could interpret overreaction as insecurity, even weakness. Nowadays, Frank would call upon a trusted runner for a dirty errand or revenge hit, erasing any direct connection to him. But, not on this night. This job was so deeply personal to Frank, it was his hit to make, his mess to tidy, his secret to keep. The crime was pure black and white, no mitigating circumstances, no apologies wanted or accepted. He needed to know the job was done properly: he craved definitive closure, both for his personal sanity and professional standing. Frank gave his head a wobble, blinked frantically to refocus his heavily dilated pupils and checked his dashboard map display. With heavy traffic finally dispersed, the LCD display read six minutes until his destination.

As he arrived in Morningside - a leafy, upmarket neighbourhood in the south west of the city, home to hard-working professionals, gym-toned MILFs, satisfied retirees, and entitled, nosy bastards - Frank knew he had to be faultless, and the sharpness of the local residents only heightened his nervous disposition. Any obvious disruption or excess noise would draw unwanted attention. Upon turning onto Bramble Place, Frank spotted some distinctive signage. He thought to himself, Nothing screams the superficial middle class more than a fucking Neighbourhood Watch. Selfless, cardigan-wearing arseholes pretending to love thy neighbour. Cunts. He drove the length of the street twice, scanning meticulously for curtain twitching coffin dodgers, zealous dog walkers and CCTV towers. It remained a wet, cold and miserable night. The famous prevailing Edinburgh wind could cut you in half if underdressed in any way.

The 3.4 mile journey had taken 22 minutes, seven minutes longer than Frank had expected. He parked adjacent to 39 Bramble Place. A spot of luck. An unoccupied parking space beneath a faulty street lamp on Hickory Gardens provided a black veil of disguise. Darkness was all Frank had known between the ages of 18 and 24. In those seven years, he'd become a fully-fledged nyctophile, but, he and others knew he was destined for bigger things. Over his 45 years, he became much more calculated in his thinking; progressing up the treacherous food chain, eventually stepping into daylight. On this night, the dark yet again settled him, it provided clarity and solace. He'd done this kind of work before as a much younger man, with little to lose and everything to gain in terms of street gravitas and reputation. But this hit carried notable risk. As a well-known man, there was a real danger that Frank would be recognised and exposed.

Frank was no stranger to run ins with the police, but this was one occasion he definitely didn't want to draw their attention. They frequently prodded for leads, occasionally launched investigations, and on three occasions, attempted to press charges. But, Frank and his expensive legal team were just too sharp for the clunky methods and processes of the constabulary. In some ways he pitied them: good people, doing good jobs, hampered by a broken criminal justice system.

Nowadays, Frank presented himself as a strait-laced, middle-aged businessman, whose dealings were all strictly above board. His growing property portfolio and rising bank balance were the stuff of dreams to most people. The granular details of exactly where his original wealth came from remained unclear, but certainly didn't involve HMRC. Yet, until the autumn of 2023, Frank's only court appearance and subsequent conviction, was the result of an unpaid speeding ticket that he simply forgot to settle.

Frank enjoyed pressure, the more important the decision, the more he seemed to thrive. Whilst he always had the ability to switch from saint to sociopath, it was never something he liked doing. Tales of a deranged, violent Frank had helped to build his public profile, but in recent years he'd operated as a meticulous planner and strategist. Continued financial success and eventual universal respect had allowed Frank to mellow and mature over time, or so it seemed. His transition from nocturnal street runner to 'legitimate' businessman had been a 28 year process, underpinned by a tonne of grit, opportunism and determination.

Adversity never troubled him; previous failings and misfortune had sharpened his character judgement and situational criticality, and he could still intimidate and freeze a room through presence alone. "If the look is cold enough, you shouldn't need to growl, if the growl is menacing enough you'll never need to bite," a typically assured Frank proverb. This was of course in relation to his own evolution; he was now top boy in every area of his life, facilitating and orchestrating all business dealings from his 1.1 million pound home, close to the New Town. He was clean, he was untouchable, and he appeared to be in complete control.

Tonight, however, he felt far from in control. He took some deep breaths to regain his composure. He glanced at his Rolex and waited for it to click past 7:58pm, he then slowly scanned right to left in all three mirrors before reaching into his glove compartment. The time wasn't random, Frank knew 7:58pm was creeping towards the start of golden hour: toddlers snuggled up in bed, prime time soaps and dramas on TV, wine o'clock on the sofa to relax and de-stress after a manic weekday. This, along with the bitter autumnal weather, convinced Frank that he had all the required camouflage and cover to pull this one off seamlessly. *No cunt's peering out their window or going for a walk in this pish,* he thought. Frank had always been a straight up details man. But, this hit hadn't been properly thought through. He'd only learned of the horrible truth 11 hours previous. This would be a crime of passion, pure retaliation and retribution. Yes, it was rushed and unstructured, but it had to be done, zero time for uncertainty, worry, or doubt. One last check in his rear-view mirror. Frank reminded himself of professional standards: no provocation, no argument, no conversation. In, clean job, out, move on.

CHAPTER 2

A KNOCK AT THE DOOR

Bath time was James Riley's favourite part of any day. It was the definition of unconditional love. Charlie's infatuation with water games filled James' heart with such contentment. Charlie had turned five years old on the 6th of September. His mummy would have been so proud of the fun-loving, carefree little boy she had co-created. Physically, Charlie was a miniature version of his daddy, with his deep hazel eyes, gleaming smile, adorable cheek dimples, and curly, chestnut hair. But all the qualities that truly mattered came from mummy: his resilience, his curiosity, his caring nature, his love of learning, his unrivalled energy. In James' mind, Charlie was pure perfection. He often questioned if he was truly worthy of being his father, and whether he could successfully raise him by himself.

Since Rachel's passing in October 2018, James had experienced prolonged and insufferable mental health episodes: depression, stress, anxiety, imposter syndrome, to name a few. A lonely and seemingly never-ending voyage of self-discovery ensued. To onlookers, James was an adoring father, he was coping in his own way after postpartum tragedy. After an extended period of compassionate leave, he appeared to be functioning well as a commercial architect, and, was adapting to life as a 37-year-old widower. Generally, most would agree that he had overcome the worst and was beginning to look to the future. But truthfully, he hadn't got over Rachel's passing. He never would. No woman would ever replace her and he had no intention of even trying. Much of the time he merely existed, barely surviving every hour of every day. James was so thankful for Charlie; he daren't think of life without him, would be meaningless, hopeless, and unbearable. Over time, James had mastered how to masquerade as his former gleeful self. He called it 'his best fake smile.'

On the day Charlie was born, James made a promise to himself and Rachel that he would be ever-present in Charlie's life, unlike his own father. In James' childhood, forgotten birthdays and no-shows at sporting events were common fuck ups. And then, when James was just 13 years old, his father decided to walk out for good. His father's primitive parental skills and peripheral existence had a major impact on James' self-belief and emotional resilience. Despite performing well in school, university and employment, James continually questioned his own abilities. He craved male reassurance at key points in his life, and was determined to make sure Charlie grew up knowing just how much his daddy loved and rated him. Even if James was in full implosion mode, he always embodied pure positivity around the boy. Charlie was blissfully unaware of his dad's deep-seated issues and many crisis triggers, he simply lived and loved his innocent young life.

Autumn and winter were the toughest seasons for James. Limited daylight and frequent bleak weather did nothing to lift the sad, dark cloud that continually man-marked him. Grief and darkness were a deadly combination, James was well aware that they often resulted in increased apathy and self-loathing. But, Halloween was fast approaching; Charlie's favourite time of the year, and James just had to step up. Charlie loved the mystique; the creepy atmosphere, the varied costumes, and of course, the mountains of sweets and chocolate. James would often try to feed off his son's infectious enthusiasm, it was the perfect positive distraction. Several months back he'd admitted to himself that the rest of this life might just be him living vicariously through Charlie, and he was okay with that. If his boy was thriving, James was satisfied.

In preparation for Trick-or-Treating, James had decked their beautiful Victorian home with ghoulish but child appropriate black and orange decorations. The high ceilings and ornate coving within 39 Bramble Place provided additional gothic charm. As a hyper-protective dad, James felt Charlie was still a little young to walk the streets of Morningside at night, and Charlie seemed to understand and accept that. Charlie just loved the excitement of visiting guisers appearing at his door and performing for his pleasure. Despite his almost permanent depressive state, James was besotted by Charlie's sheer innocence and purity; he was his lifeblood, his mood booster. Both had agreed to scoop and carve pumpkins together in the morning. Paired activities were such a joy for the always effervescent Charlie; for James it provided uninterrupted connection, teachable interactions and paternal purpose. He often had to hold back tears when undertaking developmental tasks; tears of fatherly pride, mixed with tears of widowed sorrow. Provided James could hold it together as dad, their bond seemed utterly unbreakable.

As he splashed and laughed in the bubbly bath, an excited Charlie asked, "Who do you think will visit this year daddy? A monster? A vampire? A werewolf?"

"Hopefully all of them son," James replied.

James plucked Charlie from the warm, soapy water and wrapped him in a luxury cotton bath towel. He gripped him in a snug and tender bear hug; kissed him on the right cheek, and murmured,

"I love you more than bats love blood."

Charlie giggled loudly.

"You're the best daddy. You're silly, but the best."

Shortly after, James dressed Charlie in comfy ghost pyjamas and fluffy green dinosaur socks. Charlie was reminded that he really should be sleeping by now. He responded, "I've left Mr Sheepy downstairs daddy."

"No problem little pal, I'll go get him" smiled James. Mr Sheepy was a constant in Charlie's life, a little black faced Suffolk sheep, bought by James, as a prenatal gift to Rachel. His once brilliant white wool was now latte beige but that's how Charlie liked his favourite comforter kept; unwashed, imperfect and recognisable at all times.

James trotted down the carpeted staircase, leading to a luxury parquet floored hallway. With a gentle anticlockwise turn of the mounted dimmer switch, white light turned to night light. He briefly glanced at the large wall clock adjacent to the staircase, the time read 7:59pm. James then leaned through a doorway on his right and flicked off all the light switches in the kitchen, signalling the end of a very long working day. He then turned, crossed the hallway and entered the living room. James plucked the tatty Mr Sheepy from the corner sofa. As he did, he heard a loud, aggressive knock at the front door. James paused mid-movement and wondered who it could be. Extended family members never visited during Charlie's bedtime routine. They rarely visited at all. He hadn't ordered anything online recently, and if he had, all his delivery drivers knew to press the circular brass bell to the right of the doorframe. James cautiously stepped forward into the vestibule and opened the elaborately carved Victorian door with a degree of caution.

CHAPTER 3

A CLOSE CALL

Thursday, 26th October 2023.

The prolonged drive home had at least given Carol McLaughlin time to reflect and process the day's events. For six weeks she'd been working with a 13-year-old boy called Jamie from the north of the city. Every Thursday they met, accompanied by his hollowed-out, methadone dependant mother, and a shattered, overloaded welfare officer. Jamie and his mum had only been reunited in the summer, after she'd managed to get clean and stay clean. The boy was a direct product of social injustice, personal ignorance and inappropriate content exposure. He'd regularly accessed violent porn on the uncensored X, he'd been groomed on the glittery Instagram, and coerced on the vanishing Snapchat. Most damaging of all, he'd recently been videoed performing a sexual act on another, unidentifiable minor whilst under the influence of alcohol. A stream of threatening WhatsApp messages followed, forcing him to steal from school peers to raise blackmail money. Eventually he broke and disclosed every detail to Carol. When neither Jamie, nor his mother reported to their scheduled meeting, Carol raced to their home address, alerting the police and social services en route.

Two police officers were able to force entry into the dingy flat at 12:10pm. Weeks of unopened mail jammed the front door at 45 degrees. Inside, Carol discovered the mother, sprawled across the tatty living room sofa. She lay comatose, snoring like a pig despite streaming sunlight and a blaring TV. As the officers checked the other rooms, Carol wadded through an ocean of empty pizza boxes, crumpled chip shop paper and mouldy polystyrene containers. The rancid smell of long decaying food made her gag. Beside the sofa was an ash stained glass coffee table, swamped with crushed lager cans and rusted lighters. The mother was fully clothed in a food stained tracksuit. She stank of stale smoke and fragrant marijuana. A knotted gentleman's tie, and an empty, darkened syringe lay by her feet. Carol grabbed the woman's skeletal shoulders and shook her forcefully.

She yelled, "Tina, Tina, wake up! It's Carol"

Her eyes barely opened, "What's up, what's happening?" A pathetic whiny response. One of the officers shouted from another room, "Carol, he's in here, we've got him."

In a panic, Carol ran to the bathroom. One of the officers was comforting Jamie, who was blubbering on the grotty floor. He had cut his left forearm with a rusty razor. Blood dripped from his elbow, filling uneven grout lines. At discovery stage it was impossible to differentiate between a cry for help and a failed suicide attempt. One thing was clear, the mother and son pair needed significant support, more than Carol and her team could offer. She couldn't help but think of her own family. Jamie was a year younger than her daughter Sarah. On her 11th birthday, Carol and her husband Martin, made the difficult decision to pull her out of her local state school. They'd hoped that the private sector might be able to protect her from the seemingly endless number of negative, even dangerous social distractions. They weren't sure if it would work, but they were willing to try anything to support their daughter's education and development.

Carol was a career long child psychologist. It was a job she used to love. Indeed, she had excelled in her role for over 20 years. In that time she had helped thousands of young people to challenge their own, and others fixed mind-sets. Empowering them to embed consistent mental and emotional coping strategies. Those first two decades brought her genuine satisfaction and pride, positively impacting those most vulnerable in society. But, since the mass distribution of smart phones, and the inception of mainstream social media, Carol began to feel her powers wane. A catastrophic swell in adolescent mental health problems in the most deprived areas of the city had rendered the service obsolete. Extreme peer pressure, unrealistic ideals and artificial aesthetic expectations had poisoned many insecure minds. In the last eight years, Carol had morphed from a white knight figure, who could offer early intervention and bespoke support, into an 11th hour unqualified shrink. Very often she felt like the last line of defence versus teenage self-destruction. Whilst the boy was a shocking case, he was far from an isolated incident. She wasn't sure if she had the stomach for much more.

Carol felt shattered as she pulled up outside 51 Bramble Place, she was grateful for the final parking space on the sodden street. She had hoped to be home for 5:50pm, just the two hours late on this occasion. The journey had been treacherous. Torrential rain and surface water had slowed and panicked most drivers on the always unpredictable Edinburgh City Bypass. She worried that her boy, Jeff, would be disappointed in her. He hated when she was late for a training night. On Thursdays they liked to run before dinner, not after. She had called ahead to instruct Martin to get him ready, they'd take off as soon as she was back. Carol had ignored two incoming phone calls on the journey home, one at 7:37pm, the other at 7:39pm. The caller was one of her weekend running buddies, her contact number humorously saved as Brian's mum. In the last few years, the pair had grown close, but Carol wanted and needed some peace and quiet after such a harrowing work day.

Once parked, Carol checked her wing mirror and waited for a green Range Rover to splash past, it felt uncomfortably close. *Jesus! Just as well I didn't open my door in a hurry,* she thought. She then braced herself for the elements and jumped out of her grey Ford Kuga and raced inside, using her work coat as a makeshift umbrella. She was relieved to see an understanding Jeff standing in the kitchen. He was still buzzing to go a run with his mum. She popped her soaked work shoes on top of the hall radiator, then sprinted upstairs, throwing on the first weather appropriate clothing she could find. Both runners were out on the road for 7:55pm, the quickest of quick turnarounds.

CHAPTER 4

THE MAN IN BLACK

The large wall clock chimed 8:00pm as the front door fully opened. James was met by a tall, sodden figure, dressed completely in black. The strangers body was covered by a slick polyester neck-to-knee trench coat. His feet waterproofed by a classic leather Chelsea boot. Frank stood motionless in the kind of horizontal Scottish rain that could penetrate a duck's downy underlay. He remained stoic as the chilly water dripped from the tip of his nose to the classy path tiles below. Subtle tones of distant traffic were replaced by the eerie sound of silence, exaggerating the rhythm of falling rain drops. Frank resembled a standing corpse, his lifeless face staring directly into James' soul. Time appeared to slow as the night drew even darker. His creepy, intimidating presence returned James to an immediate state of emotional numbness and confusion.

Frank's soaked head and face were completely uncovered; he was maybe two metres away, but even in the poorest light he was identifiable. Albeit, James had never seen this handsome but broken looking man before. James wondered if the man in black was drunk, drugged, or both. Had Frank accidentally blown his own cover by forgetting a balaclava or mask?
Did he just not give a fuck?
Or was this all deliberate?
Perhaps he wanted James to see his facial expression, or lack of?
Ultimately, only Frank could answer these questions.
"Can I help you?" James asked, uneasily.

"James Riley?" Frank whispered. In truth, he didn't even have to ask. A quick glance was enough to confirm that this was the man he was looking for. "Yes." James replied, softly. Frank robotically raised his right arm, exposing a 9mm automatic pistol with an attached silencer. James took a sharp intake of breath, his body froze on the spot. No more words were required at this point, both men knew what actions were about to follow.

Frank fired silently towards both thighs, delivering a single bullet above each kneecap. James dropped to his knees like a wounded soldier in an epic war movie. His strained, contracted body remained within the vestibule area; he couldn't run, he couldn't even move. James emitted a pitiful whimper, as a single tear trickled down his left cheek. Frank had transformed into full executioner mode; no messing about, no mercy given. His demonic eyes seemed to revel in the punishment, widening and darkening post impact. The stricken James couldn't process whether his body and brain were reacting to pain or terror, likely a combination of both. Since pressing the trigger, Frank hadn't moved an inch. His presence was gargoyle like, towering over James with a dreadful, evil stare.

Resembling some sort of twisted experiment, the excruciating pain felt by James briefly transcended into near pleasure. Since Rachel's death, he'd been left numb. Other than his loving interactions with Charlie, James had been rendered a functioning zombie, living day-to-day without emotion or feeling. This heinous attack had awoken something from within him. The pointing of the gun had startled him. The somatic pain had facilitated long forgotten feelings of hatred and hostility. Despite his desperate state, James felt alive, possibly more alive than at any other point in the last five years. He stared directly back at Frank, taking in every single detail of his murderous, vengeful face. James' tortured expression seemed to unsettle Frank for a very short time, his eyes weren't full of regret or remorse, as he would have expected from a guilty man. Indeed, James' loathsome upward stare could easily have been misinterpreted for desire, such was its intensity.

James was still gripping Mr Sheepy in his right hand; his grip only tightened as the sharp, hot sensation continued to worsen above both knees. Being in possession of Mr Sheepy filled James' mind with a sickening sense of apprehension. Any warped feelings of possible pleasure had been and gone. Would young Charlie come searching for his prize asset and expose himself to the shooter? *Please god no!* The gruesome scene had an agricultural feel to it; like a shotgun wielding farmer, standing over his prize ewe who'd been mortally wounded during a complicated lambing. There was a real sense of inevitability about James' fate. Frank looked like he was enjoying the power he held over his incapacitated adversary. The defeated James felt flooded by anger and bewilderment, and a host of unanswered questions. He thought to himself, *slaughtered on my own doorstep by a man I've never met, for a reason I don't know. Fuck this life!*

James was used to psychological distress. He'd already been pushed beyond the limits of many. He tried hard to remember any personal fuck ups that could warrant such a punishment. He'd never been involved in drugs or gambling, and hadn't been intimate with a woman for over four years. Professionally he had a strong delivery record, despite many mental challenges. James attempted to recall any work related errors he had made, in a final attempt to shed some light on this mindless violence.

Had he missed a deal-breaking deadline?
Had he messed up planning on a multimillion pound job?
Had he unwittingly stole money from a business or company?

Whilst at his lowest, James had supported Edinburgh City Council on a consultancy basis regarding the design, construction and final costings of the new Meadowbank Sports Centre. To his knowledge, they'd regarded him as a credible and respected contributor, who had worked effectively with all stakeholders. No toes stepped on, no enemies made, no corruption that he knew of. James was at a complete loss.

Was this mistaken identify?
Did the shooter have the wrong address?
Perhaps James was guilty of something? Had the anguish and stress of losing Rachel brought on undiagnosed amnesia or dementia?
Why couldn't he think? Why couldn't he remember?

James knew it had to be payback for something major, but he simply couldn't conclude what. The only thing that was clear to him was the central role he was playing in this physical nightmare of hellish proportions. His thoughts continued to spiral. James' despair was twofold. His murder would signal a shockingly premature end to fatherhood. A deeply disturbing conclusion to an already tragic tale. He'd also never know if Charlie was safe, loved, nurtured and successful in this life. As Frank took aim at James' torso to deliver a third, and most likely fatal blow; he noticed a small, vulnerable looking figure in the middle ground of the darkened hallway. The minor had clearly creeped cautiously downstairs as the sinister Frank went about his work. "Daddy!" Screamed Charlie. James' heart broke the second he heard Charlie's voice. A horrific situation just got worse.

The boy's introduction conflicted Frank. He hadn't been warned that a child would be in the house. *Do I really finish this bastard in-front of his boy? Do I kill them both?* After some prolonged brain fog, Frank steadied his thoughts and his right hand simultaneously. His bitterness and thirst for revenge returned instantly. "Sorry boys, but no cunt fucks with Frank Smith." Frank took a sizeable step forward with his right foot, the distance between the two men was now one metre. Both made direct eye contact for a final time. Frank gently squeezed the trigger again. As he did, James twisted his head and torso slightly to his right to scan for Charlie's whereabouts. He attempted to shout one simple word, "Run!" The trigger muted James' call; discharging a final bullet from chamber to barrel, travelling through the silencer attachment like a lightning bolt, finally entering James' chest from almost point blank range.

James remained in a kneeling position. Some seconds later, his upper body slumped forward towards the floor in a slow, lifeless motion. Charlie sprinted as fast as his little legs would allow. He jumped and cuddled into his daddy like a neglected puppy, longing desperately for affection and reassurance. He grabbed James' right hand, but immediately panicked as he made contact with a saturated Mr Sheepy, now claret in colour. Charlie peered upwards towards the shadowy shooter. In response, Frank gave a menacing grin, that the devil himself would be proud of. The brutal blackened figure then turned at funeral pace and walked into distant darkness. Charlie's uncontrollable tears matched the deluge of rain outside. The time clicked onto 8:02pm, a monster had indeed visited 39 Bramble Place.

CHAPTER 5

THE BOTCHED JOB

Frank had nailed the slow-paced, atmospheric walk off. Upon turning, he unscrewed the silencer, slipping the pistol into his right coat pocket, the silencer into his left. The narcissist in him wished there had been an audience to recognise and appreciate his cold, killer instinct under pressure. He casually scanned left and right for window movement; all clear. He felt a visceral rush of pure adrenaline, something he'd missed since going 'legitimate.' But, Frank's arrogant swagger soon turned into a hurried walk, which developed into a slightly panicked jog, and finally, a very deliberate sprint back to his parked Range Rover. Once at full pace, he moved like a clumsy toddler; hopping, skipping and jumping over deep puddles. The sheer volume of falling water meant that both lower legs got dunked. The severity of the situation started to sink in, and quickly. Frank's brain spinning like an old washing machine full of banging trainers. Initial feelings of euphoria and closure satisfaction morphed into emptiness and self-doubt. He'd just murdered a much loved family man, and respected professional on his doorstep, in one of Edinburgh's most premier postcodes. This would be national news. *Fuck.*

Soaked to the skin, Frank sunk into the driver's seat. After a prolonged inhale and exhale, he berated himself. *Stop being so fucking soft, you're Frank fucking Smith.* He reached over the central console with his left hand to close the opened glove compartment. Rain water dripped onto the leather passenger seat from inside and outside his coat. He remembered he'd left a black windbreaker jacket in the footwell. He used it to wipe rain water from his eyes. With a sharp finger jab, he reawakened the V8 animal from under the Belgravia green bonnet. He then indicated right and hurriedly pulled out of the snug parking space.

"Oh ya cunt!" A still dazed Frank hadn't checked his driver side wing mirror and was blasted by a loud and prolonged car horn. Both vehicles had avoided contact by a matter of centimetres. He thought to himself, *That's the last thing I need, a fucking crash.* Frank shook his head and awkwardly raised an apologetic hand. After a three second stand-off, the other vehicle drove away, Frank wasn't sure if the startled driver had glared back at him or not. He gave himself a moment to settle and refocus. He then checked all mirrors and scanned his now conscious blind spot, before re-entering Hickory Gardens. He was homeward-bound. Mission almost complete.

As he drove quickly, Frank began to question many of the actions and decisions he had taken that evening. He chastised himself for his shoddy overall performance. *Big Rambo would have executed that far better than me.* John 'Rambo' Jeffries, a trusted old associate, who had completed literally hundreds of tasks for Frank over the last 20-odd years. As Frank journeyed northbound on Lothian Road, more intrusive thoughts troubled him. He began ruefully ruminating about 'Hitman School - Basic Training,' and wondered if he'd properly fucked it for himself and his family...

- *A good hitman goes full incognito mode. FAIL*
- *He scans for bastarding video doorbells. He'd installed one in his own house. FAIL*
- *No witnesses ever live to tell the tale. FAIL*
- *He doesn't run away, emotionless at all times. FAIL*
- *A getaway driver should be used; as should an acquired vehicle, nothing owned. FAIL*
- *Leaving the scene must be inconspicuous, no commotion caused, no attention drawn. FAIL*
- *A professional brain is a clean brain, no substance misuse. FAIL*

Frank would never have made these fundamental errors as a switched-on runner. Had he lost his frontline edge over time? Yet more wasted seconds spent on unfounded, exaggerated and muddled self-criticism. *Nonsense!* he concluded, slapping his forehead with his left palm out of pure frustration. Should he have taken more time to strategically plan this hit? Could he have used big Rambo as a cool-headed getaway man? Yes on both counts, but, he had to act, and act he did. Anyway, what was the point in moaning? *You can't undo what's already done,* Frank thought to himself. He now had to grasp this new opportunity and look to rebuild what James had destroyed. That process would begin as soon as he reached his own front door.

Literally two minutes from home, there was another mad panic for Frank. The traffic lights on Menteith Road had trapped him. He sat impatiently, his chiselled but aging features exaggerated by the red glare of stop. Frank was acutely aware that another vehicle had pulled up alongside him. Peripherally, he noticed two contrasting colours; blue and yellow. From the corner of his left eye he could make out a Battenberg pattern. *Fuck!* Two bearded male police officers occupied the front seats. They turned right in tandem and scanned Frank's gorgeous Range Rover. He felt like he was being frisked through sight alone. "Look forward, chill out," mumbled Frank through gritted teeth. But he couldn't help feeling paranoid. He could imagine their conversation...

"He looks nervous, Do you think his tyres are maybe balding?"

"Maybe. Look at his eyes. He looks like he's drunk. Or taken something."

"Incredible car. I wonder how he got the money for that."

"I'd guess drugs. He does look pretty panicked."

"Thank god" sighed Frank. The marked police car continued straight as Frank cautiously turned right onto Morrison Street. He demonstrated the nervous diligence of a learner driver; mirrors, signal, manoeuvre. Yet another near miss.

Frank had agreed to call Amber when he was a minute from home. She answered after a single ring, confirming that she'd been eagerly awaiting contact. Frank didn't speak initially and was met by reciprocated silence. After five seconds of nothingness; a soft, quiet and nervous female voice asked, "Is it done babe?"
"It's done," replied a sombre Frank. "Unlock the back door and get me a black bin bag".

"Sure thing," she responded. "I've poured you a whisky and I'll get you towels for a bath. You focus on you, I'll get everything else cleaned up." On arrival, Frank turned off the ignition and made one further phone call. "Jo pal, it's Frank, listen, Lucas has been a little restless going down, it might be closer to 10:00pm by the time I'm there, that okay? Right that's great, see you then, bye." He then jogged into the pitch black rear garden, passing through the unlocked garden gate. He stripped in the pouring rain, knowing fine well he couldn't risk transferring any DNA evidence into his home. If he was to remain untouchable in terms of law enforcement, the events of Thursday, 26th October 2023, had to be erased and completely untraceable to him. A naked Frank ran straight to the upstairs bathroom. Task one, thoroughly scrub hands and finger nails. Amber wrung Frank's sodden clothes at the back door and threw them in the black bag. She was instructed to leave his coat, he would clean the pistol and silencer once washed and settled.

CHAPTER 6

RUN FOR YOUR LIFE

Jeff and Carol were two-thirds through their leisurely two kilometre run. Over the last seven years the pair had become addicted to running. Their infectious personalities had encouraged many others to become fitness fanatics too. The wind and rain never bothered them; if anything, extreme weather simply added to the immersive experience. Jeff and Carol were close to inseparable, outside working hours you very rarely saw one without the other. Both had a passion for the great Scottish outdoors and shared the very same zest for life. Unlike many others his age; Jeff loved the wetter and darker months, his long, shiny black coat brought warmth and protection against all elements. Carol looked to match Jeff's cosiness as temperatures dropped and rain frequency increased. A fluorescent bobble hat and reflective rain jacket were essential items for cold night running, both provided her with further shelter and safety.

For Jeff, vigorous exercise made him feel so carefree and alive. For Carol, it had always been the perfect stress release from work. Personality wise, Jeff was his mother's spiritual doppelgänger, she'd brought him up so well. In fact, their only significant difference was physical appearance; Jeff had been adopted by Carol and Martin when he was only nine weeks old. In a new life, full of favourite memories, Sundays were Jeff's personal highlight. He and Carol would always complete one of two challenges; a 5km park run, or an early morning leg burner up Arthur's Seat. In the summer months that meant a summit sunrise as early as 5am, and the most gorgeous view of the city's iconic panoramic skyline. The pair would often spend a couple of hours simply taking in the surrounding beauty of Edinburgh. Carol and Jeff had met literally hundreds of companions along the way, all sharing the same common interests of fitness and friendship. Indeed, Jeff had met his best mate up Arthur's seat a few years prior. After their weekend exercise routine, the pair always returned home for a warm shower, hearty brunch and quality family time on the sofa, accompanied by Martin and Sarah.

Thursday nights were always treated as a 'loosener.' A quick jaunt around the block to ready the legs for tougher weekend trail work. As both drenched runners turned right onto Bramble Place, Jeff was convinced he'd heard someone in distress somewhere in the nearby distance. He stopped in his tracks, his eyes squinted as he consciously tried to listen through the pounding rain. He glanced back at Carol but she hadn't reacted in the same alerted fashion. Jeff had been praised a thousand times in his life for his exceptional hearing and listening skills. He thought to himself, *fuck this, I'm going to investigate*. Jeff exploded from a standing start, he sprinted like he'd never sprinted before, leaving Carol in his puddle vapour. Carol shrieked, "Jeff, come here!" She had recently celebrate her 50th birthday, but had the body and endurance levels of a 30-year-old athlete. However, when Jeff got going, no one could match him.

Whilst moving at top speed, Jeff listened intently to ensure he was on the money destination-wise. As he got closer to the moans and wails he knew his instincts were correct. After a 400 metre continuous sprint, Jeff took a sharp right turn onto a stunning Victorian pathway which led to the opened olive green front door of number 39.

What he then witnessed was bizarre and disturbing in equal measure. The scene was befitting of a Halloween horror movie set. A little boy sobbing over an adult's crumpled, still body. Someone had lost a tonne of blood, presumably the adult but it was hard to tell on first inspection. A breathless Jeff ran to their side, both were instantly recognisable to him. He could hear a faint gargling noise coming from the James' mouth. He was clearly very-badly injured, Jeff tried to wake him up, but no joy. He'd missed the grizzly incident by a matter of minutes, maybe even seconds.

Jeff knew he needed his mum, and quick. He tilted his head back, nose to the sky and began barking and howling as loudly as he possibly could. His front paws bouncing off the ground with every guttural woof like sound.

Carol was on scene maybe 90 seconds later, but to Jeff it felt like a lifetime of noise production. As she reached the black and white tiled pathway, she gasped. "Oh my fuck, what's happened?" Little Charlie was in no condition to respond; he was shocked, and so deeply sad. He wept as he clutched onto his fallen father. Carol laid James flat and checked for a pulse. She then hastily dialled 999 on her mobile phone and gave every required detail to the operator. She held Charlie's right hand in hers as she spoke. She had never gabbled with such speed or unease. She hung up the phone, dropped to her knees and pulled Charlie into a hug, cradling the boy she knew so well. "It's okay Charlie, it's okay baby, I've got you." Charlie snuggled in tight, the chilling experience would haunt him forever, but, in that very moment he felt safe in Carol's rather damp arms.

Almost apologetically, Carol took off her hi-vis soft shell jacket and covered the blood soaked James in a desperate attempt to keep his broken body warm. She then hurriedly text Martin whilst cuddling Charlie. She didn't want to panic the boy further by making another descriptive phone call. Carol was joined by four concerned neighbours who'd been alerted by the echoing Jeff. They further covered James with sofa throws, providing more warmth and comfort. They didn't dare step inside number 39 in fear of further contaminating an obvious crime scene. Instead they chose to dash around in the teeming rain, covering the throws with bin bags to keep them dry before reaching the vestibule. A modesty screen was erected using three locally sourced clothes horses and four overlapping and tightly pegged bed sheets. The scene resembled that of a wounded racehorse, receiving veterinary treatment during a treacherously wet national hunt meeting.

Jeff's loud and prolonged barking had now attracted many other residents. A supportive and sympathetic crowd began to gather in the street; despite the continuous, heavy rain. Initially, it was only Carol who understood the full bleakness of the hideous scene. For Charlie's sake she wanted to paint a positive picture following the sordid shooting. "Daddy's just relaxing baby. You wait 'til the paramedics get here, they are real life superheroes. Daddy will soon be as right as rain, okay?"

Her final comment encouraged a courtesy smile from the crestfallen Charlie. Wiping away a personal tear of pride, Carol stated, "Very soon, daddy will be in a warm hospital bed, surrounded by the very best doctors in the world. And you, you'll be snuggled into big gentle Jeff on our cosy sofa. Once I've towelled him dry that is."

"That sounds good," Charlie said, faintly.

Martin arrived out of breath having jogged from number 51, balancing a number of dampened blankets and towels to help compress and staunch the three serious puncture wounds suffered by James. Martin was an adoring husband, he'd do anything for Carol, well, almost anything. This was undoubtedly the most unexpected and shocking request of their 20 year marriage. A Principal Teacher of Biology, Martin was confident enough to inspect each contact point with a very small degree of credibility. The perforated chest wound in particular was terrifying. Martin leaned over James' chest and quietly summarised in Carol's left ear, "I'm no medic obviously, but the bullet seems to have smashed his sternum and the medial side of his shoulder blade looks badly damaged too. As for heart, lungs, ribs and spine, who knows?"

The blown exit wound on James' back was maybe twice the size of the neater entry wound on his chest. Blood continued to leave James' body at a steady rate, Martin hastily tried to plug and mop with limited success. For a final time, he leaned over and whispered to Carol, "What the fuck is going on here darling? Shot through the legs and chest? This is a fucking execution."
Carol shook her head in disbelief, "I have no clue Martin", holding back tears as she responded. Charlie continued to cuddle her tightly. Everyone waited patiently for an ambulance crew and police team to arrive, each minute that elapsed felt like an hour. During a poignant moment of reflection and near perfect silence, Jeff thought to himself, *if he survives this, I must be due a fucking belter of a treat.*

CHAPTER 7

ANGELS COME IN MANY FORMS

The time had just struck 8:26pm, a flashing beacon signalled the arrival of a speeding ambulance. Every dripping car windscreen illuminated by vibrant blue. It had been exactly 20 minutes since Carol called. The emergency crew's presence brought a small sense of hope, and a huge sense of relief to Carol and Martin, who had done everything they possibly could as medical laymen. They had done their best to save their neighbour, holding it together long enough to do what was needed, but ultimately they knew they were just guessing. Indeed, it was only really Jeff who had the natural skill set and back breeding to reliably undertake his key role. Flat-coated Retriever's being renowned for their athleticism, hunting ability, pointing accuracy and protective character. Oh, and they love water, in any form. It had been a concerted effort from all, but had their amazing instinctive efforts been in vain? It was time to step aside and let the skilled professionals get to work.

The worried crowd dispersed from the front of the tiled path in a typically choreographed middle class fashion. This created a neatly funnelled passageway towards the maimed James. His body remained partially covered by the homemade modesty screen; the variable wind strength providing snapshot glimpses of blood as the sheets flapped and fluttered intermittently. Next to arrive on the scene were three police vehicles; two marked, one unmarked. A striking mid-40s brunette, exited the driver's side door of the unmarked car. Immaculately dressed in a chic black mac jacket, bottle green polo neck, skinny black jeans and black leather Dr Martens. Her name was DCI Taylor, she was all business, and hugely comfortable in this very uncomfortable situation. DCI Taylor energetically directed and coached her officers like a top flight football manager, delivering a rousing and thought provoking pre-match team talk. Her officers were willing pawns and carried out every instruction with impressive efficiency and speed. Needless to say, in all investigations the opposition hold a significant initial advantage. From there, the police need to find ways to equalise, and ultimately attempt to score the winner through solution focused detective work. If they didn't already know, DCI Taylor's presence confirmed to the now tens of onlookers and well-wishers that a significant criminal act had taken place.

As expected, the paramedics approached James in an assured and professional manner. They descended like guardian angels; assessing, diagnosing, treating and consoling with such nurture and empathy. Carol quickly described how she had moved James, in perhaps a naive attempt to make him more comfortable. Martin described the three bullet wounds as best he could. He wasn't too sure how helpful his input had been, but the crew thanked him nonetheless. The calm yet hurried nature of the crews work, and the noteworthy medical detail they were frenetically sharing, clearly highlighted a race against time. James was stretchered into the ambulance at 8:52pm, some 50 minutes after the clinical chest shot. It departed as quickly as it had arrived, sirens blaring to clear the now busy street.

A desperate Carol questioned Martin, "Do you think they'll be able stabilise James?"

"I'm not sure honey, he's in a bad way. Let's pray the surgical team at the Royal Infirmary can save him. No one can be confident of a positive outcome though."

After giving initial witness statements, Carol and Martin were free to go home. They both agreed that the hospital was no place for a discombobulated little boy, pining for his daddy to wake up.

They therefore decided that they would look after Charlie until a member of his extended family got in touch. Neither were sure when, or if, that would happen. The horrible circumstances around this impromptu sleepover would never be erased from memory, but at least Charlie would feel loved and secure in familiar surroundings.

Carol picked up Charlie and held him tightly to her chest, he reciprocated by wrapping his arms over both her shoulders. She tenderly whispered, "Time to go to your favourite place, let's make a hot chocolate." Carol walked with Charlie in her blood soaked arms back to her family home just after 9:10pm. The unforgiving wind and rain continued to slow their progress, but it was only a three minute wander. Carol's ears were ringing and she felt numb, physically and figuratively. She wondered if she might be entering a state of shock, but she tried to stay focused. The last thing Charlie needed was for her to lose it now. The forever loyal Jeff was with them every step of the way, playfully wagging his tail as if nothing had happened. Martin had run ahead to make toast and marshmallow topped hot chocolate for all human members of the family.

When they got home, Carol took Charlie upstairs and into the en-suite shower. He sat stock-still as the cascading water soaked his thick, curly hair. Carol remained in a trance like state, her protective movements and actions were completely instinctive. She vigorously lathered and rinsed Charlie's hands and forearms with shower gel to remove the now drying and flaking blood of his father. The white shower tray was stained momentarily as blood and water emulsified, before racing down the large chrome drain simultaneously. She covered him in a large beach towel and held him close - partly to dry, partly to console. Little did she know that just over an hour ago, James had held Charlie in the same moist hug, but the emotions could not be more different. Mr Sheepy had opted for a bath over a shower. Martin provided him with a luxurious 60 degree hot wash and spin programme. He would be back to brilliant white in a matter of minutes, allowing him to return to support and comfort duties.

After showering, Martin encouraged Sarah to interact and engage with Charlie. They had played together hundreds of times in the past. But, it seemed that Sarah had perhaps outgrown Charlie and was content in her own private space with her new smart phone. *That fucking phone,* thought Jeff. He too had lost a dear friend to technology; morning hugs and chase games had been replaced by continuous, mind numbing, thumb scrolling of Instagram and TikTok. Three weeks before, Jeff was forced to pee in the kitchen because Sarah was too fucking lazy to come away from a shitty influencer video on YouTube. How degrading! He hadn't had an accident in the house since he was a pup. Jeff had moaned and whined for minutes, but the once caring Sarah didn't move a muscle. Glued to her screen like a technology junkie, hooked on likes and emojis. The average dog only lives between 10-13 years; every single day counts for them, if only human owners fully understood that. Perhaps they would reciprocate their furry friends' unconditional tenderness and attentiveness if they did. What a way to live.

Jeff was the definition of dog tired. *Saving lives is a tough shift,* he thought. He wanted to stay awake to further protect his dearest humans but his eyes were heavy and glazed, every blink a step closer to slumber. He cuddled into the now warm and snug Charlie, who was sipping on an indulgent hot chocolate, topped with fluffy, sticky marshmallows. Bluey and Bingo offered a welcomed distraction, Charlie grinned from ear to ear as he stared attentively at the TV. Just as Jeff's chin slowly lowered and rested on the black leather sofa, he was alerted by a loud and authoritative instruction. "Sarah, sort Jeff out with a treat honey, he's been the best boy tonight." This was it! Jeff propelled himself off the sofa, landed on all fours and bolted towards the kitchen. What would be an appropriate treat for such a heroic intervention? *Fillet steak, cooked chicken, even some grated cheese would be magnificent,* thought Jeff. He sprinted towards the utility room with unbridled enthusiasm. He then slammed on the brakes and clumsily slid across the laminate kitchen flooring towards his destination. Jeff eventually halted 30 centimetres from his ceramic food bowl.

Oh for fuck sake! You kidding me on?

In seven years he'd never felt so underwhelmed or undervalued. He'd been confronted by a bowl of desert dry salmon kibble.

Fuck you Sarah, fuck you! He yelped internally.

That's the last time I switch into full retriever mode for you whorebags! And get off that fucking phone!

An utterly despondent Jeff sauntered silently back into the living room and hopped back up beside his little pal, resting his chin on Charlie's left thigh, which was covered by an oversized dressing gown. A settled Charlie smiled and began to stroke Jeff's left ear. Jeff let out a huge sigh, he was still pissed off at Sarah, but at least Charlie appreciated him.

Carol had watched Charlie grow up on Bramble Place. Since Rachel's passing, she invited him and James to Christmas dinners, Easter lunches and summer barbecues at number 51. James had been Carol's neighbour for eight years. In the three years prior to her death, Rachel and Carol had struck up an incredible bond. They quickly became best friends; both were fitness fanatics, both loved socialising and shopping, both adored their immediate families, and were excited about everyone's life chances. Partly due to the significant age gap, Rachel also regarded Carol as a life mentor; replacing the wine dependent mother she endured growing up. Carol read a self-penned poem at the couple's humanist wedding in 2017; it captured them perfectly, both as individuals, and, as a loving couple. It was like she'd known them forever, she was closer than family. Following Rachel's death, Carol was selected and announced as legal Guardian to Charlie in June 2019. A title she loved, and a responsibility she embraced with enormous pride and affection. James and Carol were close when

Rachel was alive, their friendship only grew stronger after her passing. James just loved how caring Carol was, she epitomised the role of Guardian, a title selected as a non-religious alternative to Godmother.

Martin kissed Carol on the forehead before heading upstairs to bed at 11:45pm. Charlie had been sound asleep since 10:30pm. A weary Carol wandered back outside to her car, dressed only in fluffy pink pyjamas, and Martin's size 12 carpet slippers. Luckily, the wild wind and rain had eased. She'd accidentally left her laptop in the back seat after parking up from work. She'd be taking the next day off to care for Charlie, but would still be expected to reply to sensitive emails. She also assumed there would be further police questions to answer, either face-to-face, or over the phone. "Phone, shit." Carol remembered that she hadn't returned the missed calls from Brian's mum. She hoped she was okay, but didn't have the focus or energy to call her back. Two main reasons for this... 1. Brian's mum can be a nosy cow and loves a bloody question, and 2. It was just too late in the evening and her mind was full. She hadn't been left a voicemail or text message so Carol assumed it was non-urgent. She'd make a point of calling her back in the morning. As she closed her car door, Carol tentatively peered down the street towards number 39. A forensics tent had been erected on the front pathway, and further police barrier tape cordoned off the surrounding area. She returned to the house, flicked off all the main lights and table lamps, and quietly made her way upstairs. She paused at the landing to check on the youngster, who was occupying their spare single bedroom. She was so fond of Charlie, he was a faultless little boy in her eyes. Carol whispered, "Night boys, love you both." As if in response, a groggy Jeff lifted his head from the shadows. He stayed by Charlie's side all night long, the ultimate protector.

CHAPTER 8

THE ALIBI

Driving a blacked out Ford Ranger, Rambo pulled into Frank's private driveway and parked beside an abandoned Range Rover. He'd been given strict instruction from Frank to arrive at 8:40pm. The forever reliable Rambo was never early or late to a job. Whenever Frank needed him, wherever that was, Rambo would be there, bang on time. Some of Frank's more gallus street runners referred to the big man as 'Shakira' for this very reason. Any piss taking was always delivered in Rambo's absence though, he wasn't the type of man you'd ever want to antagonise. Frank warned the morons of the group that Rambo's father was in actual fact a Belgian Blue bull, his mother an African White Rhino. To his amazement, some of the dim-witted cunts believed him, but that was the effect Frank could have on naive, eager to impress types. Rambo had never worked out a day in his life, never taken a protein supplement, never jabbed a steroid; but had traps, deltoids, triceps, biceps and pecs most full-time gym monkeys could only dream of. At 6 foot 2 inches tall, and 17 stone of lean, powerful, aggressive muscle, you'd need a 44 magnum to stop him in full flight. Frank proudly referred to this as "Beast mode genes."

The only man brave enough to ridicule the physically imposing Rambo to his face was Frank himself. He used to joke, "He's not very bright, but he can lift heavy things." Rambo accepted the crude insult, it reminded him of the rung position he occupied on Frank's leadership ladder. Any other man would have lost his nose for such insolence, but, Rambo knew it came from a place of love. He'd always felt that Frank and him were much more than associates, to him, they were best friends. As Frank's ambitions grew, so did Rambo's admiration.

They first met as teenage footballers back in 1994. Rambo started out as a doting teammate, he was mesmerised by Frank's self-assurance, both on and off the pitch. From there, Rambo developed into an obedient street runner. No job was too big or too intimidating, he'd walk through fire to impress Frank. A 14 year journey led to Rambo being recognised and eventually respected as Frank's professional fixer. He was convinced he would have ended up just another scheme rat without Frank's constant guidance and support. Frank brought structure, purpose and even security to Rambo's life. But, Rambo had far more capability than anyone, other than Frank, gave him credit for. He was so much more than a street hardened heavy.

Frank could change personality at the drop of a hat; sometimes nurturing, challenging and questioning within the very same sentence. He was the ultimate extrovert who could talk business or pleasure in any crowd. Not Rambo. He lived to serve, he lived to please. He wasn't comical, he rarely spoke and barely smiled. In truth, Rambo's limited words and expressionless face only added to his aura. His scale and athleticism, combined with a cyborg like stare gave killing machine vibes to any outsider. His imposing walking gait exaggerated by clacking drover boots and clenched fists. Yet, he remained completed submissive to Frank. Rambo fully appreciated that in this life there are leaders, and there are followers. And he would follow Frank faithfully until the very end, without a single challenge, question or doubt in his mind. Frank knew, that if he provided a clear chronology, simple orders and concise details, there weren't many jobs Rambo couldn't set up, fix or resolve with military like precision and zero traceability.

By 2016, Rambo had completely outgrown the title of 'fixer', he was pretty much Frank's right hand man, and had a simplified overview of many business operations. But even Rambo didn't know about the actual details of this particular job, this one was bespoke to Frank, for good reason. The only articulated details were, "Memorise the story, be at my bit for 8:40pm, bring your cleaning products." The secrecy didn't bother him though. Sometimes the boss shared everything, sometimes he shared nothing, which was his prerogative as the top man. Rambo took enormous pride in every task assigned to him by Frank. If this specific task was a simple retrospective clean-up, so be it. Rambo got to work on the Range Rover. It was probably an hours job but Rambo knew he couldn't cut corners, every speck had to be lifted, and every droplet had to be wiped. Just then, a sudden knock at the driver's window. Amber needed access to the double garage; she signalled for Rambo to reverse the Range Rover away from the front door. As always, he politely obliged.

Frank lay in a deep, warm bubble bath. As his body slowly defrosted, he consciously reinforced his alibi for the evening, ensuring there were no plot holes. The sharp, refreshing scents of vetiver and bergamot provided some much needed clarity to his thoughts. He had arranged a late night meeting on George Street with a well-established business acquaintance, Joseph Zimmer. Amber knew the the chain of fictional events inside out; Frank ate dinner with her and their son Lucas at 6:30pm, he then played with, bathed and settled the boy for 7:45pm. Frank then took a shower, before checking his departure time from Edinburgh Airport early the following morning. Between 8:25pm and 9:15pm he prepped for his meeting with Joseph and packed hand luggage for his business trip. Flight tickets had been bought 14 days previous. The routinely scheduled trip to Amsterdam was never intended to play a major part in any alibi but added real solidity to the fabricated narrative. Frank then playfully chatted with Amber before setting off for George Street at 9:45pm. He drove his Range Rover Overfinch which had sat idle in the driveway all day as he worked from home. He'd been preparing a bid for two town houses in Leith Docks. Provided he'd got lucky with traffic cameras and CCTV, it was the perfect bullshit production.

Meanwhile, in the real world; Rambo was busy sponging, dusting, polishing and hoovering the SUV. The time was 9:19pm. Frank had bought the vehicle some four and a half years ago, this was the first time Rambo had ever had to do a deep clean on it. In a months time Frank would be replacing it with an upgrade. Rambo reached into the glove compartment, he knew the pistol had been stowed there pre-shooting. Every inch of the cabin had to be squeaky clean, spotlessness equalled innocence. An embarrassing discovery followed, as he stumbled upon an unused, expired condom, still sealed in its silver foiled wrapper. It almost appeared to be acting as an improvised bookmark, wedged inside the vehicles owner manual. Classic Rambo though, he didn't question, he didn't judge. He simply helped his boss out by disposing and forgetting. Finally he cleared all previous destinations from the vehicles satnav and completed a full system reset. Once finished his cleaning duties, Rambo called it a night. He opened the front door of the house and shouted upstairs, "That's me done Frank, thank you." Rambo thanked his boss at the end of every day, a clear and consistent display of appreciation.

A refreshed Frank appeared at the top of the stairs, dressed in another beautifully tailored suit. He looked to have regained his swagger. He casually sipped a single malt from a crystal glass in his right hand. "Thanks pal, I'll call you when I'm home from Amsterdam." The relaxed instruction was accompanied by a reassuring wink. But, a probing question followed. "You definitely tidied everything yeah? Needs to be immaculate."

"Yeah boss, all good. Cleaner than a strippers pole.

"And what time is it Rambo?

"Just gone 9:35pm boss."

"Good man. Right speak soon."

As Rambo departed, Frank peered out of his expansive living room window, whisky glass still in hand. Rain water continued to cascade down the large panes of toughened privacy glass. As he scanned the secluded rear garden, Frank made out a dancing flame from underneath his large solid oak gazebo. Next to the flame, a stunning female silhouette. From Frank's perspective, the image resembled that of an alluring séance.

Amber stood over the orange heat, she was further warmed by a black nylon jacket, and tightly wrapped woollen neck scarf. She was close enough to enjoy the warmth on her beautiful face, but far enough away to remain safe. This was common behaviour from Amber. She loved that most viewed her as Frank's ditzy blonde, the facade was completely deliberate. Passive-aggression and puppet-mastery were areas of specialism for the angelic Amber. The flames licked and eventually caught the black bin bag that contained Frank's incriminating clothes. She smiled as she sipped on an ice cold glass of Pinot Grigio, watching satisfyingly as her man's clothes burned, melted and cindered away to almost nothing. She'd used a full tin of lighter fluid to make sure every damp garment ignited. Amber knew that Frank had to be on Flight KL1276 at 5:50am the following morning. Provided take off went smoothly, everything was about to fall into place.

After finishing his whisky, Frank returned to the back door, carefully wiping the pistol and silencer with a fresh set of gloves and washed hand towel. Back upstairs, he used bore oil and a cloth pull through to meticulously clean the barrel, giving the impression that it hadn't been fired. The pistol and silencer was relocated inside his password protected security safe, underneath his dark oak office desk.

Amber watched Frank do a quick check of Rambo's valeting skills, he left the house at 9:47pm. Shortly after leaving, her mobile rang. It was Frank. "Mind my coat is on the black slate patio, make sure you burn that too."

"No problem," she responded.

After burning a final item, Amber finished her wine then returned indoors. She removed her jacket, but the scarf remained firmly in place. She'd worn a different scarf every day for almost a week. The next half hour was spent pottering around the house. She wiped down worktops, dusted every wood surface, then steam mopped all hard floorings. Amber liked a tidy home, it settled her, it relaxed her, it gave her a sense of belonging. The incredible 3000sqft house she was standing in, served as a timely reminder as to why she put up with so much shit. After a moment of deep reflection, it was time for self-care and pampering; a long, relaxing shower, followed by a face mask, another large glass of wine, and her favourite drama series. She checked Lucas' baby monitor before making her way upstairs.

Amber walked into the ensuite bathroom. She turned on the shower and began to get undressed. She unbuttoned her shirt, slipped off her jeans, and removed her underwear. Naked from the shoulders down, she stood and stared into her oval shaped vanity mirror. Using her right hand, she began to slowly unravel the woollen scarf, circling her head anticlockwise as she did so. As the scarf fell to the floor, so did a solitary tear from her right eye. Five day old bruises were revealed. She could still make out each individual finger mark either side of her trachea. The extensive yellow and purple bruising resembled a galaxy of stars in a twilight sky. Amber felt nauseous, gently placing both of her hands around her neck. She remembered vividly the unbearable pressure, her eyeballs bulging through pain and panic. But, it wasn't the brutal affliction that haunted her, it was the control. Having someone else dictate your next breath was terrifying; she had been completely defenceless, utterly powerless. Amber blinked her eyes rapidly, and returned to the present. She took a deep breath, turned slowly, and stepped into the steaming hot shower.

Frank returned from his meeting with Joseph at 11:33pm. To his surprise, Amber was still awake. Typically she'd be in bed for 11:00pm on a weeknight. She was irritably pacing up and down the living room, arms crossed right over left. A pensive look was etched on her face.

"You okay?" asked Frank, as he threw his key fob onto the glass faced kitchen table.

"Have you seen the fucking news Frank?" A panicked, exasperated whisper.

Frank paused, uneasy. "No, why?" Amber responded sarcastically, her voice close to breaking. "Well, lucky for you, I've recorded it."

Frank walked into the living room, picked up the television remote and pressed play.

"An adult male is currently fighting for his life after a major police incident here in Morningside. Neighbours reported a disturbance just after 8:00pm this evening. Ambulance crews and police teams were quickly on the scene. Detective Chief Inspector Charlotte Taylor has appealed for any witnesses to come forward. Initial reports suggest that the adult male is in a critical, unstable and life-threatening condition in hospital. More updates as and when they come to us. Stuart Paterson, STV News."

Frank's heart began pounding, perspiration gathered on his forehead, his mouth instantly drying. He gulped aggressively in a conscious attempt to stop rising vomit. "How the fuck is he alive Frank?" Frank turned to his right and snapped. "Shut the fuck up Amber, fucking shut it! I did this for you. I was protecting you, and all you can do is fucking moan!" The now imposing figure of Frank stood over a trembling Amber, like a school bully demanding lunch money from a poor little soul. "Unless this cunt's The Terminator, there is no way he is surviving the night, alright? Now fuck off to your bed." Amber responded, "Fuck off? Why? What have I done Frank?"

"You know exactly what you've done, cunt."
Amber looked back at him, confused. "I don't know what you mean," she whimpered.
"Don't act thick. I found your shite gear. Sitting on the fucking kitchen table, right where our son eats his breakfast, builds jigsaws, draws pictures. Get out my sight you fucking tramp."
Amber ran towards the staircase, sobbing as she ascended. The sudden disturbance abruptly woke Lucas. He was disorientated and distressed. Amber entered his room and gave him a huge hug. The inconsolable consoling the inconsolable. She knew the youngster would settle through comfort and reassurance, unfortunately, her suffering would likely continue.

As silence returned downstairs, Frank replayed the news report maybe five or six times, absorbing the details; "Critical", "Unstable", "Life-threatening". Surely James was a dead man? Surely? He fucking had to be. James knew Frank's height and build, he'd seen his face, he'd heard him speak. A wave of nausea engulfed Frank again. He whispered, "Did I give him my fucking name?" *Surely not*, pondered a forgetful Frank.

Amber lay in bed, quietly crying. She maintained the foetal position throughout, facing the far wall, she couldn't bear the thought of turning and facing Frank. Frank entered the bedroom and lay on top of the duvet cover. Holding his phone in both hands, close to his face, he constantly hit refresh on two separate news apps until the clock hit 1:00am. Once James was confirmed as dead, he could relax. Maybe news would come in the morning? Neither he, nor Amber would sleep much that night. Frank didn't even bother taking his suit off, he lay on his back staring at the ceiling. Not once did he try to touch or speak to Amber. He had to be at the airport in three hours. Frank thought to himself, *stick to the plan, nothing changes.*

CHAPTER 9

SUMMER LOVING

Friday, 17th June 2011.

A bronzed 20-year-old Amber Shields touched down in a dreary Edinburgh. A baggage cart aquaplaning through a deep runway puddle was a stark reminder of Scottish summertime. She had been touring sun-soaked Australasia as part of a transitional gap year. She'd sampled a variety of customs and lifestyles in an action-packed nine month trip. It had been an immersive experience, free from the pressures and expectations of her pushy family. Her father, Alistair, hadn't wanted her to go travelling at all as she'd already repeated a year of schooling. This was a direct consequence of the family's relocation from London in May 2006. However, Amber's fun-loving and rebellious nature meant that she got her way.

Whilst travelling, she felt unshackled, it was the perfect opportunity to live completely carefree. Indeed, she might not have returned to Scotland at all if it hadn't been for her constantly demanding and, at times, possessive father. After negotiations, he had agreed a one year deferral of academic study. He knew that any more "Fanciful gallivanting" would result in a reneged offer from the university. This would have been a personal embarrassment to him, he'd harped on about the brilliance of his daughter since she was a toddler.

Amber hadn't been keen on a family reunion. The older she got, the more insufferable her father became. He was an arrogant prick, the type who could talk at you for hours without asking a single question. He was loud, obnoxious and money-hungry. She sought comfort in the fact that her homecoming was only for the summer holidays. She would also be returning to her barista job for two months, further limiting family contact time.

The previous year, she'd been scouted and signed by a modelling agency. That opportunity was her mother's dream, not hers. Amber was simply the willing subject in front of the camera. But, after much deliberation she decided against taking on any work. Partly because she couldn't be fucked listening to her moaning foghorn of a father, ranting aimlessly about female objectification. Oh the irony. Making coffee for strangers was just much less hassle for all.

Come September, Amber would be embarking on a five year Medicine degree in Aberdeen. There, she could enjoy further parental distance. Sure, she'd keep in touch, but the thought of not having daily dealings with her father was a pleasing one. She hoped Aberdeen would be a fresh start, a place where she could live independently in peace, without the constant pressure of having to impress the overbearing Alistair. She hoped to forge her own adult pathway, one that she chose, and was passionate about. Amber's mother, Gayle, had agreed to pick her up from the airport at 8:35pm. Amber was pleasantly surprised that her mother was... 1. Available, and 2. Compos mentis, at such a time of night. Typically she'd cut a lonely figure; curled up on the sofa, in a darkened living room, listening to repetitive classical music, about to uncork another bottle of Sauvignon Blanc.

Amber had never wanted to move to Edinburgh. She was so happy living in Hampstead. She loved her life there, and had a wonderful network of friends and teammates. She'd been privately educated at an exclusive all-girls day school, and was an exceptional artist, sportswoman and academic. At that time she had the looks, talent and mindset to excel in any elite profession of her choosing. And that was so often Amber's problem: almost every choice was made for her, particularly in relation to her future.

The sole reason for the forced move was her philandering father. She resented him for it, she always would. Over time he'd destroyed her mother. Gayle was once a glamorous woman, full of self-assurance and charisma. Alistair had reduced her to an insecure wreck, who'd lost almost all trust and confidence due to repeated cheating and gaslighting. Gayle couldn't bear the public shame of a failed marriage or messy divorce so agreed to start again in a new postcode. She'd hoped to write an alternative family narrative in a different location. They eventually landed on the elegant neighbourhood of Stockbridge, Edinburgh. Alistair promised Amber a 'Hampsteadesque' vibe, great schooling and lots of top-end sporting opportunities. He promised Gayle a fresh marital start, and a chance to prove that he was a worthy husband. In truth, he was a grade A twat. At the time of relocating, he'd simply ran out of staff to run his private dental practice in Hampstead. He'd fucked half of the local female receptionists, the other half he'd thoroughly creeped out.

Amber knew that moving to Edinburgh was simply an opportunity for Alistair to branch out and find 'fresh meat', whilst trying to make a shit tonne of money in an affluent area. Although the thought of more adultery wasn't a conscious fantasy at the time, a predatory leopard never changes its spots. Amber was fully aware that things wouldn't improve. She'd been ripped away from friends and peers, all so her arsehole father could break her mother's heart 100 times over.

Back in 2006, she'd tried desperately to reason with Gayle, attempting to rebuild her as a fierce, powerful and sexy woman over several weeks. Facilitated by morning runs, lunch dates, and movie nights; Amber advocated that they could survive and excel together, as a strong mother-daughter duo. Despite her extraordinary maturity, she was still only 15 years of age, and, ultimately, she was unable to challenge her mother's broken, pessimistic thinking. After yet another extramarital affair, the move to Stockbridge went through.

Travelling was pure escapism for Amber, as was moving up north. Yes, she liked the idea of being a doctor, but hadn't really given it huge thought. She always felt that university life was more about experimentation and self-discovery, than burying herself in endless books and studies. Alistair; part-time dentist, full-time wanker, was keen for her to follow in his footsteps and take over the family business longer term. But, a now streetwise Amber wasn't interested in dentistry, or impressing her father, or following his example in any way. In truth, Amber's first love was art. That would have been her preferred vocation, had it not been for the constant criticism and pressure. She cringed thinking about the forever judgemental Alistair, berating her throughout her senior school years. One fatherly quote in particular had been forever etched in her mind, "You think I've invested thousands of pounds in your education for you to draw fucking pictures? I don't fucking think so, girl."

Smiling, Amber threw her luggage into the boot of her mother's black BMW X3. Whilst being back in Edinburgh for summer 2011 wasn't her ideal choice, Amber had always felt incredibly close to her mum. Both were genuinely delighted to see each other. She jumped into the passenger seat, reached over, and gave Gayle the biggest hug. Although recent affection was more linked to pity than love. "Hello mummy, how are you?" Squealed Amber.

"I'm good baby, look at you!" The pride in her mother's voice was audible. Amber had left Edinburgh as a girl and had returned as a woman. A confident, beautiful and glowing woman. She had always been a big character, her next question pulled no punches. "You chucked or castrated that clown yet?" A cheeky grin accompanied the disobedient remark. "Amber please, you've only just landed honey. Your father and I are actually doing okay, thank you very much. He's changed since you've been away, I promise. Play nice when you see him, please?" A critical Amber responded, "Mum, you are so fucking soft; he's a prick, always has been, always will be. Women are just objects to him, he'd shag a barber's floor if you forgot to sweep it." Gayle almost exploded with laughter. Her response perhaps should have been an angry yelp or embarrassed tears, but there was just something about Amber's delivery that always made Gayle laugh. Her life was so much fuller with Amber in it. She appeared to be a force of nature, the full package.

No man or boy seemed safe during the summer of 2011. A mischievous Amber honed her puppet-mastery skills in the classy bars and clubs of Edinburgh's George Street. She appeared to be a sultry dream, but was a nightmare for the victim's credit card the following morning. Accompanied by her stunning school friend, Olivia Henderson, they hit the town on most Friday and Saturday nights. For eight weeks straight, they slayed tens of handsome males, neither woman spending much at all in the process. Both flirts used humour and suggestive eye contact to entice and tempt unwitting playthings. Perma-tanned fuck boys, tattooed athletes, smooth businessmen, cute students: no one could escape the magic of Amber and Olivia. They were utterly captivating. If, and only if, you passed every test, over a prolonged period of the evening, you might get to see the sunrise with one, or both. But their selection process was incredibly thorough, these ladies were class acts. No pricks allowed in the bedroom, they could spot a bullshitter or a cheater from a mile away...

Q1. Are you single?
Q2. Why and how long for?
Q3. What do you/what will you work as?
Q4. What are your hopes for the future?
Q5. How important is family to you?

The pair worked like black widow spiders; enticing potential mates, hand selecting partners, then killing it dead. No full names disclosed, no numbers shared, no Facebook following. Of course, the men and boys returned to the very same bar, the very next weekend, for another bite of the forbidden fruit. But, Amber and Olivia were too elusive for that nonsense. They were already working on their next set of victims in other classy establishments. The perfect design.

To Amber and Olivia, the summer of 2011 was all out ecstasy; harmless, no strings attached, experimental fun. Typically, they would chat to attractive strangers about education, football, holidays, cars etc. and then stick or twist depending on sexual chemistry and quality of conversation. Often they would be bored stiff by one-dimensional spice boys or quick-talking, slow-listening egomaniacs. But, both agreed that free cocktails were free cocktails! Indeed, some of their funniest moments came on Saturday and Sunday mornings when they reminisced about the many charlatans and gasbags they'd encountered the night before. Totalling up their free drinks tab the next day was also a source of great hilarity. The following weekend was an opportunity to improve on their previous record.

CHAPTER 10

INSTANT REGRET

Saturday, 20th August 2011.

The night that superseded all others. The events of 20.08.11 would be imprinted on the minds of both women, as would the other individual involved. For Amber and Olivia, it was their final night in Edinburgh. On the Monday, Amber was travelling to Aberdeen. Olivia would join her parents in France, officially becoming a partner in their successful wine business. It would be the last time they'd socialise together until the following summer. They had agreed to finish with a 'bang'. Both women had a glint in their eye, there was a shared understanding that it would be a special evening. The city centre was bustling with energy and atmosphere, the Edinburgh Festival Fringe was in full flow, as was the alcohol. Amber and Olivia shared two bottles of Prosecco, the first sip passing their lips at 1:15pm, an early start. Whilst every used and abused male played a small part in their flirtatious game over the previous eight weeks, they were keen to test themselves intellectually and find themselves a 'real man' of substance for their final fling. They joked about being brave and calling out one or two men to join them for afternoon drinks in the summer sunshine.

Amber and Olivia playfully people-watched as thousands of George Street shoppers, day drinkers and festival goers wandered by. Savagely but in their minds, subtly, they comically guesstimated the cock size and bedroom fantasies of every individual who owned a penis. Age didn't save you, neither did religion, or ethnicity, or any other exceptionality, everyone was fair game. The pair laughed and giggled for hours, the more they drank, the cruder the responses. All answers were fun, some answers were pure filth. The girl' Aviator sunglasses provided a degree of anonymity for the generally unwitting walkers, but no one dared to glance back at the gazing sirens.

That was until something really captured the imagination of Amber and Olivia. Both peered over their glass frames, biting bottom lips. The synchronisation had all the hallmarks of a 1990's Diet Coke advert. It was 4:15pm; a tall, dark haired male strolled past, holding two designer shopping bags. He was smartly dressed, well-groomed and carried an air of mystery that intrigued both women. Amber and Olivia were in full flirt mode. Fuelled by Prosecco and mischief, they casually called him over. He routinely obliged as perhaps most gentlemen would. "Hello. My friend and I are playing a little game, wanna play?" asked Amber.

"Sure thing," replied the cool and assured stranger.

"Take a seat," a firm instruction from Olivia, as she removed her sunglasses.

"Eh, am I gonna like this game ladies?" asked the now inquisitive and unsure male.

Amber smiled. "We think you'll love it, but if you don't, we'll let you leave without buying us a drink, deal?"

"Deal," replied the stranger.

Olivia began. "Okay, question number one: what's your name?"

"James."

"Hello, James. Question two: how big is your cock?"

All three burst into hysterics. James couldn't quite process if this situation was real, or whether it was part of an improvised street act. He paused for a few seconds to ensure he wasn't about to be soaked, or pied, or laughed at. "Big enough," he joked. "Girls, I am sorry to be rude, but is this a wind up? I'm just doing a bit of shopping." A tipsy Amber responded, "This is everything you think it is James, just two girls enjoying their last night in the Burgh. Question three: what's your biggest bedroom fantasy?"

"Wow," a stunned James couldn't hide his emotion, perhaps even his excitement, as he sat back in his chair. "Doggy style with a voluptuous stranger I guess, but if it was two vs. one I'd maybe need some more think time". All three individuals scanned the eyes of one another, the chemistry was contagious.

Amber eventually broke the tension, "Two espresso martini's please James, and whatever you're having."

The next hour or so took a step back into normality, naturally building conversations that all three could engage in, and contribute to, without personal embarrassment or judgement from others. The random meeting was essentially playing out back to front; outrageous flirting to break the ice, then some chilled character building to form a genuine connection. It was clear to both Amber and Olivia that the 25-year-old James was a talented and well-rounded individual. He was also a successful professional, working within the city. He spoke fondly of Aberdeen as a student city, he had spent six great years there studying architecture. This pricked Amber's ears, she wanted to know everything about the local facilities and amenities. "What were the best restaurants, bars, clubs and cafes? Were there good parks, or art galleries? Were there any hockey clubs, or tennis clubs, or golf courses? Were Aberdeen FC worth watching every other Saturday?" James laughed, "I don't work for the Aberdeen tourist board, you know." Every piece of feedback was glowing though, which really excited Amber. The threesome sat for hours and hours, chatting about the present, the future, and what the rest of the night might entail. Both Amber and Olivia could feel themselves gravitating towards James. It was easy to get lost in his hazel eyes and muscular frame. Both fantasised about the body underneath his light blue cotton shirt, they tingled with excitement. It was during a bathroom stop that Amber and Olivia realised they were in serious trouble, James had sailed through their selection process. Amber whispered to Olivia, "He's only bought three bloody drinks, we've bought four." They were no longer in control.

James had never been so captivated by two younger women before. He had some doubt in his mind given the five year age gap. But decided to invite Amber and Olivia back to his one bed flat on Brunswick Street, just off Leith Walk. He figured, both were stunning young women, who seemed to know exactly what they wanted in life, and certainly knew how to use their words and bodies to seduce men. James wasn't entirely sure how things would pan out, but the situation became much clearer the second the Yale lock on his front door snibbed shut behind them.

Amber and Olivia struck like two coiled vipers, biting and licking James' neck. James completely surrendered to them, this was going to be one hell of a night for all involved. At varying points during the lust filled encounter, James had to plead for softened moans. He was conscious that neighbours might mistake passion-fuelled moans for mercy calls in a frenzied domestic knife attack. It was a greatest hits of bedroom pleasures; biting, slapping, sweating, trembling, screaming. If they had the wherewithal to video it, all three willing participants could have been millionaires overnight.

James was the first to wake in the morning, flanked by Amber and Olivia, legs intertwined. As he raised his weary head, he'd wondered for a confused second if he'd been burgled, then quickly realised how wild things had got just a few hours previous. Clothes and underwear scattered everywhere, damp sheets, a smashed lamp. *What a fucking night,* he thought to himself. He laughed as he returned his head to the pillow, waking up both women.

James offered breakfast and coffee. "That would be lovely," Amber replied, smiling dreamily. "I would love a coffee," said Olivia, yawning.

"Coming right up." James got out of bed and made his way to the kitchen. Strangely, there was no awkwardness, it was just three consenting adults, casually refuelling after the most incredible sexual experience of their lives. All three went their separate ways at 10:05am, James called them both a taxi, kissed them on the cheek, and thanked them for an unforgettable night. Amber and Olivia giggled as they hugged each other goodbye.

Just like that, summer 2011 was signed off, quite the ending! *How was university night life going to live up to that?* Pondered Amber. For the first time ever, she felt a sense of regret upon returning home. She couldn't help but feel she should have asked for James' number, a surname at least. On first impressions, the man was special. He was successful, attractive, engaging, funny, sensual, caring. Everything she thought she wanted and needed in a man. Part of her wanted to jump straight back into a taxi, and run back to his flat before she sobered up and forgot the exact location. But that would look like instant infatuation, not a good look for a 20-year-old George Street socialite. She chose to stay put. Amber reassured herself; *in two weeks' time you'll be 130 miles away smashing fresher's week, there'll be a thousand other Jameses to choose from.*

CHAPTER 11

GREEN, AMBER, RED

University life started promisingly for Amber. She moved into Hillhead Village, a bustling halls of residence to the north east of the city. Despite its dull, grey, granite appearance, Aberdeen was everything she'd hoped for in a student city. It boasted a vibrant night life, lots of sporting opportunities and genuine history and culture.

The first few weeks and months were pure joy; full throttle, eat, sleep, rave, repeat. Amber's charisma endeared her to everyone she came across. It was in week one that Amber met her best friend, the brilliant Steph. Brilliant was the only way to describe this fierce redhead from Orkney. Unlike Amber, there was a simplicity to Steph's thought process. She knew exactly what she wanted and was driven to achieve it. She had visualised becoming a doctor since primary school. The clear plan was to graduate head of her class. Her projected career would be long and distinguished, excelling as an innovative, researched informed gynaecologist. Amber on the other hand hadn't even considered a specialism to that point. Compared to Steph she felt like an imposter, who'd simply stumbled upon medicine through parental pressure alone.

From that first week, Amber and Steph had an undeniable connection. People just loved being around them, their infectious energy brought amusement to the driest of core seminars and tutorials. As a gin-guzzling double act, they captivated and impressed in every social circle. To any adoring onlooker, both young women appeared to be the definition of 'it girls.' But, despite their many similarities, it quickly became apparent to Amber that Steph had something that she didn't, something that made her complete. Steph's family circle was tight, secure and so very caring. Steph called her parents daily, often just to check-in, or to simply say that she loved them. Home visits were frequent. Amber on the other hand would actively avoid incoming phone calls and never returned home on weekends or holidays. Over time, she assumed her mother had been lost to drink. The only meaningful interactions with her father were over grading sheets. A set of documents that he demanded off the university each semester so that he could track his daughters performance in granular detail, unit by unit.

During weekends and holidays, Amber cut a lonely figure, barely leaving her bedroom. But, isolation was a preferred choice to family reunion. Many of her hours were filled by scribbling and painting on paper and canvas. Finished products acted as a clear reminder of just how talented an artist she was. Flatmates and coursemates often commented on the quality of her work. Indeed, Steph often stated that she had a "God given talent that should be celebrated and promoted." But, Amber simply palmed off positive reviews and evaluations. A demon voice in her head seemed to whisper persistently, *Daddy does not approve.* Fucking prick. One first year conversation over a cheap bottle of white wine would stick in Amber's mind forever, it provided clarity and understanding about family nurture. Steph simply asked,
"What do your parents want you to be?" Amber thought for a long time. "Anything impressive I guess. Dad wanted me to be a dentist, then eventually settled on a doctor. Mum wanted me to go into modelling for some mad fucking reason." Steph nodded her head sympathetically. "What about you?" Asked Amber.
"My parents just want me to be happy." Answered Steph, simply. Amber smiled enviously, but her response was completely genuine. "I fucking love that." A concerned Steph knew that under the smile, and the energy, was a broken young lady who was deeply unsure of herself.

Unofficially, Steph became Amber's own private tutor. She dragged Amber through much of her first-year coursework and summative exams. They continued to party hard and their connection only grew stronger. But, as time progressed, Amber's insecurities deepened. She began to hide from academic pressures, sleeping in for 9am lectures and missing submission deadlines. Her behaviour continued to deteriorate, deflecting and self-pitying in equal measure. In second-year, she famously missed the first two weeks of semester one because she was 'celebrating' Andy Murray's first major win at the 2012 US Open. The bender was followed by a shame-laden three day panic attack about returning to campus. When Alistair called to chase her up, she responded with, "Dad I've got a bad flu, give me a fucking break." It was clear to Steph that Amber was hiding from her problems and insecurities.

Weekends of isolation and painting morphed into 48 hour drinking binges. Drinking led to pill swallowing and powder snorting. It seemed the only way to escape her lows was to get high. Steph remained supportive but grew tired of babysitting her, tired of making up excuses to university staff. By the time she stumbled into third year, Amber was still searching for her 'why' in life. It seemed she'd taken every negative trait from her dysfunctional parents. Amber wondered if she'd ever find her true calling. To her, Steph was such a natural, she was anything but.

After another summer of daydreamer travelling in 2013, Amber knew that her next hospital placement would kill her or cure her, perhaps literally! For any self-driven, passionate medical student, placement is a 100mph rollercoaster that brilliantly connects theory and practice. But, for anyone who is struggling, or disengaged, third-year placement can be a head-spinning concoction of heartbreaking paediatric cases, never-ending elderly care, and monotonous pre-assessment clinics. Yet again, Amber broke under pressure. She found herself drinking off shift to forget the sights she'd seen. Often she'd take cocaine whilst on shift to keep herself sharp and attentive. It was a devastating spiral of repetition that made pressurised decision-making and problem-solving almost impossible. At her worst, she was barely surviving on three hours sleep. She felt crippled with regret and inadequacy, she'd allowed herself to be coerced into a career and a life that she didn't want. Even without Alistair pestering her day-to-day, he still seemed to control her psychologically. Amber concluded that she'd rather have no father than the one she'd been burdened with. She wanted to be free, she needed a life without negative parental influence. It was time for change. As always, she had the full support of Steph.

By the time September 2014 came around, Amber had completely reinvented herself. It was the first time she'd felt comfortable in her own skin since August 2011, the summer of James. She'd come to realise that a lifetime of trying to impress people, particularly family, was a one way ticket to the funny farm. As soon as Alistair's academic allowance had cleared, Amber took it upon herself to enrol on the four year Art History Honours programme at Aberdeen University. She could put her shit-show medicine experience firmly behind her.

Her new pathway filled her with a sense of purpose, focus and hope. Finally, she could excel in a field that she loved, working and collaborating within a professional community of equals. Challenges would of course remain, she knew she'd have periods of doubt and affliction. Drugs and alcohol were always temptations, but, she was confident in her own ability to self-regulate and eventually wean herself off both.

Her immediate concern was how she'd deal with her father, once he realised his prodigy had swapped a scalpel for a palette knife. Part of her was excited by the prospect, part of her was terrified. But, she found solace in the knowledge that Steph had her back. Together they had the strength of character to stand against him, free from stigma and compulsion.

Friday, 19th December 2014. Amber had circled the date in her diary three months previous. She'd noted down, 'judgement *day.*' An apt title as Alistair spent every day of his life judging and patronising people. She knew that semester one grading sheets would be landing in Alistair's inbox around lunchtime. It was 11am, Amber and Steph sat in a busy coffee shop on Bon Accord Crescent. They went through seemingly hundreds of scenarios, based around his potential reactions and sanctions. Steph even joked about about a call duration sweep stake, the shortest guess, 15 seconds. The longest, 25 minutes! Amber kept her phone on loud. At 11:32am it began to ring, the name on the screen, *The Tooth Puller.*

Amber didn't even bother to say hi. Her silence was met with a tirade of abuse...

"What the fuck is this? You think I'm paying for your flat and your car just so you can fuck me over by giving up on your career? I don't fucking think so. You know your problem? You're a spoiled little brat who's had everything fucking handed to you. You think you can just jump from a proper degree to this Mickey Mouse shit? Over my dead body young lady."

Amber waited for quiet. After several seconds, Steph acted as her response trigger, signalling her time to attack with two thumbs up.

Amber's response was full of confidence. "Hello dad. Listen I understand that you're upset and I get it, I really do. But, I can't keep doing this. I'm sick of being judged by a fucking job title. You and I have no relationship and I'm now comfortable with that. You've destroyed mum, but you won't destroy me. I need to do what's right for me, not you."

"You entitled little bitch!" Alistair bit back enraged. "Destroyed your mum have I? Well to avoid any repetition, Amber, we're fucking done. You know, sometimes in life you have to recognise a poor investment and just cut your fucking losses. So all the best making rent and insuring your car. What a fucking disappointment you've turned out to be."

Amber slowly lowered her phone from her right ear and placed it on the table, "Well, that went well."

Both women looked at each other and burst into awkward laughter.

"You think he'll go through with that?" Asked Steph.

"God knows, probably, I guess. As you've witnessed, he's the worst." Replied Amber. Steph gave Amber's hand a loving squeeze. "Let's cross that bridge if and when we come to it babe."

Amber responded in a soft tone, "yeah, you're right, as always."

"Come on then, this is a good day. I'll get menus, let's have lunch." As Steph left the table, feelings of doubt and dread flooded Amber's gut, she felt physically sick. She knew that Alistair could take everything away from her, just as she'd found her feet. As she stared out the shop window, echoing white noise pierced her ears. Passing cars appeared to blur, fracture and merge. She felt like she was living inside a kaleidoscope, her heart pumped harder and her breathing quickened. At that second, the buzz of her phone on the pine table startled and refocused her. Steph returned almost immediately.

"You okay pal?"

Amber replied sharply, "Yeah great, never better."

"You gonna check your phone or not?" Both the message sender and message content surprised Amber. Message from mum; "I am coming to Aberdeen on Monday. Let's do Christmas together like old times. I have the best gift for you. Trust me this time, please."

Gayle's visit gave Amber such a boost. For the first time in many years, her mother looked healthy and relaxed, she seemed happy. Most importantly, she was sober. Amber knew her mum had good news to share but she didn't want to force it, Gayle would announce when she was ready. On the Monday evening, Amber cooked a delicious dinner, they then sat down to watch a movie. Amber brought through a bed throw from Steph's room. Gayle immediately cuddled in, it was just like old times. Amber initially enjoyed the affection, but, as the night wore on she felt a lingering sense of guilt. After all, Gayle was also a victim of circumstance. Amber couldn't help but feel that she had abandoned her mother, condemning her to prolonged suffering at the hands of Alistair. Amber was no longer a little girl, perhaps she should have challenged the misogynistic prick much earlier. After entering a distracted trance, she shook her head and brought herself back into the present, focusing on the movie once more. She concluded in her mind that hindsight brings simplicity and clarity to any challenging situation.

On the Tuesday they shopped all day. Gayle treated her daughter to a new designer handbag for Christmas. They laughed and joked about old times and began to consider Amber's future as an exciting new artist. But, doubt yet again crept in to Amber's psyche. "I don't know mum. The artist thing has always been my dream, you know that. But now that he's pulled the plug, god knows what I'll do." Gayle responded with a smile. "Well, remember I said I had a gift for you?"

"Yeah, yeah. The bag, it's gorgeous , thank you so much."

"No, not the bag Amber. Consider it an added treat, somewhere to store your paint brushes."

"You see, I've actually got you two gifts, neither to do with a handbag." Amber looked at her mother, confused. "Gift one. I've finally binned your father, fleecing the bastard for 50% of everything in the process. The least I deserve for years of deceit and turmoil."

"Jesus fucking Christ mum! You little beauty! When did this happen?"

"Became official on November 6th, but I didn't want to trouble you. Steph told me how well you'd been doing and I didn't want to create any distractions. Plus, I knew you'd need to face his wrath over changing courses, and I wanted it to be a quick conversation for everyone's sake."

"Wait. What? You knew I'd given up medicine? But, I didn't tell anyone."

"And that's when a best friend comes in Amber. I've been in constant dialogue with Steph. She's kept me in the loop throughout. I know all the challenges you've been through and how they've made you stronger. I've understood your need for a change for a very long time now. Which brings me on to treat number two. I've covered your rent for the first six months. A small gallery in Frederick Street, Edinburgh. It's been fully fitted out, you just need to design and fit your signage. I've even bought a domain name for your website."

"Wait, what are you talking about mum?"

"Look. Let me show you some pictures and videos."

Amber couldn't contain her excitement. She leaped towards her mum, grabbing and hugging her with a child-like naivety. Gayle almost dropped her phone during the constriction.

Amber bounced as she spoke. "So, what does this mean mum?"

"Amber, sweetheart. It means that you have your own gallery. You don't need to worry about a thing except creating, marketing, advertising and selling great art work. This is the start of a new life, your own life. Any profits you make will go towards your mortgage."

"Mortgage? On what mum?"

"Oh, I eh, I took the liberty of putting down a deposit on a one bedroom flat, just off Comely Bank. It's beautiful, stunning, I know you'll love it." Amber became tearful, "Mum, you've saved me. You've fucking saved me. That's three treats! How can I ever repay you?"

"You're happy, that's all that matters to me now darling, that's my repayment. Now it's up to you to go smash it, and I have no doubt that you will."

'Art by Amber' officially opened on Saturday, 21st February 2015.

CHAPTER 12

ONE FINGER, ONE THUMB

Wednesday, 1st November 2023.

Rambo patiently waited outside a Pilton tenement block. His fingers playfully tapping on the steering wheel as he listened to Johnny Cash's *Cat's in the Cradle,* a song about a child's desperation to impress his father, only for the father to be too busy to care. Johnny Cash was all he ever listened to, repetition and consistency suited him.

Rambo knew the immediate area inside out and was completely comfortable in his surroundings. After all, it was where he grew up, where he initially made his name. A large group of tracksuit wearing youths loitered outside the Chinese takeaway adjacent to where he was parked. Fruity smelling vapor clouds floated amongst them. The braver types attempted to subtly look his way, before engaging in covert conversation with the others, many of whom had chosen to keep their heads buried in their mobile phones. Rambo's gleaming black pick-up was instantly recognisable to all. No one dared to stare for too long out of fear and respect.

He opened a packet of peppermint chewing gum and popped two pieces into his mouth. His first couple of chomps resembled a relaxed bull, casually chewing his cud in autumn twilight. He was expecting an important call. That very second, Johnny stopped singing and Rambo's phone started to ring. The name 'Tina' appeared on his dashboard. He answered silently. A quivering female voice said, "That's him away John."

A few moments later, a tall hooded figure emerged from a fire exit at the base of the tenement. His exaggerated strut was peacock-esque, no doubt showing off to the impressionable youngsters across the street. "The state of this cunt," muttered Rambo. A flash of headlights soon turned a cocky swagger into a nervous looking shuffle. Rambo lowered his tinted passenger window. The concerned hoodie spoke first, "Rambo, hi. What eh, what you doing here?"

"Get in", ordered Rambo.

"Look, Rambo, what's this all about? I've got places to be." Rambo leaned towards the opened window. His eyes appeared to darken and deepen. "I said get in, Robbie." A dismayed Robbie glanced back at the young onlookers, but, did as instructed. What choice did he have? Before he could fasten his shaking seatbelt, Rambo pulled out and drove away from the crowd, all four doors automatically locking as he did. He couldn't care less that people had witnessed the brief interaction. No one would ever speak against him.

"Take that fucking hood down," instructed Rambo. Robbie again obliged, continuing to stare ahead. He couldn't bare to make eye contact with the monster to his right. Johnny was now singing the chilling, *God's Gonna Cut You Down*. It was pure coincidence but to the already intimidated Robbie it felt very deliberate.

Another incoming call interrupted Johnny mid-song. This time it was Frank. Uncharacteristically, Rambo chose not to answer. Rambo turned up the stereo volume to emphasise the damning lyrics; "What happens in the dark will be brought to the light."

"Look, I am sorry, okay? Whatever I've done, I can undo it, I promise." Robbie's voice breaking and cracking with every spoken word. "Please, am fucking begging you man." Rambo pulled into Swalemoor Road, it was eerily quiet, the more he drove, the darker it seemed to get.

Robbie cried, "Where are we going man? I've got a missus and a kid, I'm only 20, we can chat this through, no?" Rambo didn't respond, he simply stopped the car.

Rambo turned off the music and reached over into his glove compartment, Robbie squeezed his thighs together and threw them to the left to avoid any contact. He wondered what the fuck Rambo was about to produce. Ominously it was a pair of large black leather gloves. Rambo slipped them on in slow motion. He looked towards his passenger and broke his own silence. "Only you can help you." Robbie's heart skipped as his eyes widened. He stuttered, "Eh, yeah, sure, I'll help me, I'll help you, no worries."

"Who's your supplier?" Questioned Rambo. Robbie laughed awkwardly. "Oh come on man, you know I can't share names, fucking hell. You trying to get me killed?" Rambo's eyes filled with menace. In an instant he grabbed Robbie's right forearm like an unhinged parent ragdolling a toddler. With one tug, he wrenched it towards his own torso. Robbie was helpless against his dominant physicality. In his right hand, Rambo held a set of electrical pliers that had been stowed in his door compartment. In a calm voice he declared, "Every time you talk pish, I'm taking a fucking digit." Then clamp! The pliers bit into Robbie's right thumb. With a machine-like squeeze, they tore through skin and flesh, before crunching and snapping bone. Robbie screamed in pain and disbelief as his severed thumb fell onto Rambo's lap. He tried to pull his arm back to grasp the gushing wound but Rambo's vice grip denied him. "Shh-shh-shh, quiet now," he whispered in a composed, sinister fashion. He waited and waited for Robbie's breathing to calm. "See, I knew that'd be the answer. So here's a another question. Who were you dealing skag to just there?" A sobbing Robbie responded quietly, "Tina."

"Tina who?" Asked Rambo.

"Tina Jeffries" Robbie replied.

Rambo interjected aggressively. "That's right cunt, Tina Jeffries. She'd been clean for 18 months, until you and those other little scumbag dealers got to her. So for that, nine becomes eight. Snap! Robbie's right index finger was now also the property of

Rambo. In complete shock, Robbie couldn't verbalise a single word of his suffering.

Rambo began his closing remarks. He'd already spoken a weeks worth of words. "Stop whining and listen good. You're gonna tell your wee cult following, your dealer pals, and your supplier that if she is sold one more drug, big Rambo is coming for them. No cunt survives, that includes your family. Is that understood?"
Robbie nodded silently. "Secondly, you are now my head of security on her boy Jamie. If he gets harassed, or bullied, or embarrassed, either face-to-face or online by anyone on this estate, you'll deal with it. Agreed?" Robbie nodded a second time. "Because if you don't, I'll be taking your right hand. Have I been perfectly clear?" A final nod from a now grey-faced, blue-lipped Robbie. "Now get the fuck out my car and phone yourself an ambulance before you bleed out. Tomorrow morning you'll tell everyone what happened here tonight, everyone from top to bottom." Rambo sped away, turning up Johnny's *Cocaine Blues* as he did. The rest of the night would be a forensic level clean up of his cabin, followed by a final check in with Tina.

CHAPTER 13

APOLOGIES ALL ROUND

Thursday, 2nd November 2023.

Frank's flight landed at 7:50am. He'd often return from Amsterdam on a Tuesday, but chose to prolong his visit on this occasion, offering both him and Amber additional breathing space. Frank had extended his stay in Amsterdam before, it didn't comprise his narrative in the slightest. He'd booked his Range Rover into the long stay car park at Edinburgh Airport, another common arrangement. In the past he'd given Amber his car for the weekend but he'd grown tired of returning to rolls of bubble wrap, empty coffee mugs and toddler toys.

The car park was a 12 minute walk from the terminal. He'd gotten lucky, driving rain and dark clouds had been replaced by a crisp frost and glowing sun, it was an enjoyable saunter. A calm Frank whistled nonchalantly as he scanned the beautiful golden trees that flanked the heavily salted pavement. Six days in Amsterdam had given him time to reflect and refocus. He recognised that he would have to apologise to Amber; some spiteful, disgusting and unwarranted words had left his lips on Thursday night. Frank was aware that he could become very intimidating, very quickly. He hoped that Amber could see it as a nervous reaction, and that he meant no threat or harm. Not this time. He had tried to call her four times in the last 72 hours, but no answer. That wasn't unusual for Amber though, she was a proud and wilful woman. She had to be to live with Frank. He was always left to sweat after an outburst, he'd have to work hard to get back into her good books.

Frank hopped into the SUV and began his short journey home. "Fuck me, how low is that bastarding sun," moaned Frank.

He squinted at distant cars through windscreen salt grime. Rush hour traffic and rubbish driving conditions equalled a slow journey. He reached for his sunglasses in the overhead compartment. No sunglasses. "Amber!" He snarled. Frank took a deep breath to settle his frustration. He was about to be reunited with his partner, it was to be a happy, apologetic occasion. Calmness was called for. But he couldn't help himself, "put stuff back where you fucking found it, not difficult is it?" Frank knew his screen wash levels had been hopelessly low, he pulled on the control stalk, more in hope than expectation. "Fucking yes Rambo!" Not only had Rambo painstakingly cleaned the interior, he had also topped up Frank's screen wash and Ad Blue fluid. Orange warning lights on the dashboard had been teasing Frank for weeks, but he'd never got round to addressing them. "That big cunt can fix anything," smiled Frank. He turned on the radio, classical piano settled him further. A tranquil and controlled version of Frank was returning home, he had a fun and relaxing afternoon ahead.

Frank called Rambo in transit. He was keen to be updated on any developments regarding the town house bids. It seemed the shooting had already become old news, he was unable to get any meaningful updates over in Amsterdam. Maybe James had died. Maybe he was dancing the fucking can-can in his living room. Frank reassured himself as he glanced at his wing mirror before overtaking a silver Ford Puma. "Just focus on controlling the controllables old boy, what's done is done." Clearly, he had a vested interest in the condition of James but he had to be subtle. Considering the high stakes, it made complete sense to keep the details of the hit in-house, exclusively between himself and Amber. Whilst Rambo had always been fiercely loyal; more eyes, more ears and more mouths only increased the chance of leaked information. Surprisingly, Rambo didn't answer. Frank could forgive the late-night missed call from nine hours ago. But, Rambo not calling back and then not answering a further time was just strange. He tried a second time, again it simply rang out. And a third attempt went straight to voicemail. *What the fuck is going on here?*

Frank arrived home at 9:09am. City centre traffic was stop-start as expected. Amber's car wasn't in the drive, that didn't trouble him. More often than not she kept it in the garage. He dropped his travel bag at the washing machine and made himself a coffee. He shouted for Lucas and Amber from the downstairs hall. Amber worked from home every Thursday and often kept Lucas off nursery. She just loved one-to-one time with him. He was her pride and joy, the greatest thing that ever happened to her. Frank shouted again, no response, the house was in silence. *Mmm, must be out shopping,* concluded Frank. He sat on the kitchen sofa, turned on the TV, and began to scan through local and national news headlines. Where the fuck was Rambo? He was his go-to man, they'd been tight for years. Why wasn't he answering? Feelings of uneasiness and irritability continued to build.

At 9:21am, Frank's phone started to ring. It was Rambo. "Thank fuck," he declared. Frank answered promptly, in a disgruntled fashion. "Where the fuck have you been?" A pause from Rambo, "Sorry boss, I was sleeping. It was a late one last night. Couple of the Leith runners fucked up on a deal and it needed fixed sharpish."

"Sleeping? Fucking sleeping?" Responded a perplexed Frank. "Listen soft lad, I need you ready to go at all fucking times, understood? When have you ever not answered me?"
Rambo sounded edgy, "Understood Frank, won't happen again, apologies." Frank jumped in again, "You're fucking right it won't happen again, and keep your fucking phone on loud from now on."

"Yes of course boss," a sheepish, childlike response from Rambo.

"Anyway, what happened in Leith Rambo?"

"Honest, some of these young boys are useless cunts Frank, few of them got roughed up bad. I'll explain later but we need to be careful, shit like last night makes us look soft."

"But it's sorted, right? Questioned an inquisitive Frank.

"Yeah it's all good now boss, no need to chase up." Replied Rambo.

Frank inquired further, "Good. Right, the Hamilton deal, tell me."

"It's been a strange few days to be honest boss. Hamilton accepted your bid on the spot; no negotiations, no bartering, cash deal, job done. Max is finalising the funds this morning, it all seemed very straightforward."

"Brilliant, I knew they'd crumble!"

"Oh, and an architect got shot on his door step in Morningside. I asked around, none of our lads know anything about it. Doesn't seem to be drug or money related, pretty random."

"An architect? Frank struggled to keep his voice steady. "Random indeed. When did this happen?"

"Last Thursday boss, I only heard on Friday."

"Is he dead yeah?" *He fucking better be.*

"Not yet boss, apparently on a ventilator. Think he was done in the chest, doesn't look good."

"Poor bastard," replied Frank. "Right thanks for the updates pal. I'll get the minutia pish from Max. I'm playing golf with him at 11:15am, he's picking me up at ten, need to grab a quick shower."

"No worries boss. Hope his driving has improved. Prick almost killed me the last time. See you soon." Rambo hung up.

Frank slowly lowered the phone from his right ear. An icy stare towards the kitchen clock. "Fuck," he whispered to himself. James had survived for seven nights. Was he about to become a huge problem?

Anxiety driven dry mouth had returned. He awkwardly joked to himself, "Who am I dealing with here, fucking Lazarus?" Frank needed a drink, something non-alcoholic, anything thirst-quenching. Walking towards the fridge, he noticed a pink Post-it note with black handwriting. The message was a welcomed distraction from his worried state. *Off to Aberdeen with Lucas to visit Steph, back Friday, love you.* A smile crept across Frank's face. Had she forgiven him already? He sniggered, *doghouse to penthouse, thank fuck.* Frank respected Steph, she was a hard-nosed bitch and a great friend to Amber. He knew she'd act as a critical ear. Frank had fucked up so many times in their eight years together. However, his Amber would always offer an olive branch, facilitating peace talks and an eventual resolution. The speed of forgiveness seemed questionable though, often it would take weeks not days.

Frank and Amber's relationship was unconventional at best, consistently volatile, and, at its worst, highly abusive. The untouchable made man cut a very different figure behind closed doors. Amber knew every one of his idiosyncrasies, shortcomings and vulnerabilities. Unfortunately for her, she was often on the receiving end of resulting rants, outbursts and worse. Over the years she had learned to live with Frank's brilliance and madness, but recognised that everyone can be broken by something bigger than themselves. Privately, Frank constantly battled self-doubt, he suffered from extreme paranoia, and trusted no one other than her and Rambo. He'd screwed over and outgrown some significant names in the last 25 years. Despite his prominence, Frank always had a feeling that he'd eventually meet his maker. Some of the things he'd seen, some of the things he'd done, were beyond comprehension to most sound-minded people. Guilt filled-memories do strange things to a man's psyche.

Deep down, Frank did appreciate Amber, or so he stated. He needed her now, more than ever. Not only was she a glamorous pin-up, she was a genuine strategist and had helped to grow Frank's profitability tenfold. She had played a key role in bringing his money into the tax system, legitimising his empire. Frank knew he had to make things right, on this occasion, a further "Sorry" wouldn't cut it.

After downing a bottle of water, he called Amber's favourite steak restaurant on Argyll Street. A reservation for two on Friday night, 8pm. Most would have been laughed at given the short notice, but not Frank. "That's you booked in Mr Smith, we look forward to seeing you again."

"Many thanks," responded Frank. He checked his watch, "Shit! Shower time." He hurriedly jogged upstairs.

CHAPTER 14

WELCOME HOME

Max Rankin tore through the elegant streets of the New Town in his Mercedes SL. Rush hour had been and gone but traffic was still fairly heavy. He drove like Formula 1 driver, pushing his grand tourer to the limit, accelerating quickly and braking sharply in a mad sprint to the chequered flag. Any passenger would have found the experience more than a little unnerving. His general behaviour was comparable to that of a beagle puppy; excitable, sociable and very loud.

Max always looked forward to his monthly game of golf with Frank. On this occasion, the chosen course was the world famous Muirfield, in nearby Gullane. Thursday was visitor day, Max had booked 18 holes and the two course carvery lunch. From his perspective, it was a chance to provide financial updates and discuss future investment opportunities, whilst building trust with the boss. He was very keen to get his belly rubbed after finalising the Hamilton deal in Frank's absence. Unfortunately for Max, Frank had worked him out years ago; an over confident, smarmy little prick who would sell his granny to make a pound. Max knew exactly what Frank needed him to know, nothing more, nothing less. To be fair to Max, he could wash and hide money better than most, and his addiction to a flamboyant lifestyle guaranteed his long term loyalty. He was Frank's dependable, if not slightly annoying financial puppet.

As Frank's operation grew, so had Max's wallet. A recent cash bonus had helped him to purchase his three bedroom flat in Tollcross. Despite his nine year run as accountant, Frank was always keen to keep Max at arm's length. At a New Year's dinner party, hosted by Frank and Amber, the cocky little shit had joked to Rambo, "I make this whole thing tick big man, you won't make real money without a good numbers man." Naturally, Rambo relayed the bold statement to Frank. Frank saw Max's arrogance as an opportunity to pull rank immediately. During his vote of thanks, he highlighted the importance of respect and integrity within the business.

"Let's get one thing straight folks. Never forget how far you've come and who put you there. A huge thanks to all of you for your contributions this year. And remember, being able to read numbers is a skill, being able to read people is an art. Cheers." Everyone had raised a glass, responded with a cheers and smiled respectfully. Everyone except Max. He felt like an embarrassed child, lesson learned and fully accepted. He'd be less cocksure around Frank in the future.

Amsterdam had afforded Frank some much needed reflection time. He had already begun contingency planning, just in case his worst fears came true. There were a number of outcome based scenarios spinning around in his head. From his perspective, some had a simple, happy ending (an obvious acquittal). Some were messy, and would require significant input from his trusted stakeholders and handsomely paid legal team, led by Craig McCracken KC. Some were a fucking disaster, guilty as charged, game over, life over.

- Scenario 1: The hit was successfully completed. Neighbours didn't see or hear anything. James never regains consciousness and dies in hospital. The kid is a blubbering, unreliable mess. Any defence lawyer's ultimate fantasy.
- Scenario 2: As above, but the driver on Hickory Gardens somehow managed to memorise Frank's private plate immediately after the near collision. A good defence lawyer's wet dream.

- Scenario 3: The kid was switched on. He was competent enough to positively identify Frank. The driver had asked their passenger to take a picture of Frank's plate using their mobile phone. A good defence lawyer's unsettled dream.
- Scenario 4: The razor-sharp kid could pick Frank out of a 20 man line up. A game dog walker spotted him sprinting to his car. The driver recognised Frank personally, perhaps an old foe. A good defence lawyer's nightmare.
- Scenario 5: The kid was fucking Rain Man. Shaggy and Scobby-Doo were out walking in the pissing rain. The driver was Miss Marple. James rises from the dead in hospital. They all witnessed and retained every detail. Save your money, no need for a good defence lawyer.

Frank stood over his ball on the first tee; the expansive Muirfield course had a farm like feel to it, acres and acres of undulating fairways and thick rough that resembled a heavy hay crop. A quick scan of the distant bunkers and a couple of practice swings prepared him for his first shot. Golf typically brought out a more relaxed version of Frank. Max was keen to capitalise on this. Standing three metres back, he proposed a cheeky challenge. "Right Frankie boy, what we playing for?" Frank bit immediately, "Frankie boy? Who the fuck you talking to junior?"
Max giggled nervously. "Relax! Only kidding boss!" A smiling Frank responded, "Match play format, and for your cheek, £100 if you win, £200 if I win. Frank was just about to launch into his backswing when Max interjected again. "Going with a three wood are you, I'd definitely hit a long iron on this hole."

Frank turned sharply, club in right hand, pointed directly at Max's face. "What have I told you about talking too much?" Max raised his hands like a bank clerk held at gun point. "Okay, okay. Serious business chat from now, I promise!"

Frank readdressed his ball, he took in a deep breath to help visualise his shot, backed up with some positive self-talk. "Left-hand side of the fairway, open up the green for your second shot. Then proceeded to shank it way right into thick rough. Max gripped his teeth tight, desperately trying not to laugh or snort. Frank looked at him in the eye and joked, "I've always thought Muirfield would be a great place to hide a body." Max giggled again, nervously. He thought to himself, *stop trying so hard, relax for fuck sake.*

Luckily for both players, Frank's game improved from hole two onwards. As hoped, the iconic course design, scenic surroundings and fresh sea air allowed his brain to relax and rest. He even managed to birdie the 4th hole, one of the hardest par threes in golf. Strangely he was enjoying Max's banter and the match play format meant that a disastrous hole wasn't an issue. Frank played golf like he lived his life, high risk, and high reward. He led by two holes as they approached the 14th tee.

"Right, let's get into it then, Hamilton deal, all done, yes?" Frank's question was almost rhetorical but he was keen for facts, figures and timescales. "All documentation is with the lawyers now boss. By next week, everything will be finalised. I only went 5% over the asking price and fully expected them to reject it. But, since we were buying both plots, the deal seemed to make sense for everyone."

"Good work, Max." Frank responded, feeling more settled. "You know, I've been thinking Max, I need to start planning for the future. I want you to set up an off shore account for Lucas. £500 transferred every month, fully accessible on his 18th birthday."

"Yeah, no problem, I can sort that tomorrow."

"And fire 50k into the S&P 500, in his name, Lucas Jude Smith."

"Sure thing. Everything okay boss?" A day dreaming Frank responded, "Who me? Oh, yeah, I'm eh, I'm fine pal. Simple contingency planning, that's all. A dad's got to look out for his boy." Frank went on to win by a single hole. Max was largely relieved at the outcome, and was more than happy to part with his money.

Max and Frank enjoyed a beautiful lunch. In between starter and main course, Frank instructed Max to call Damian Grant. Damian was an experienced member of Frank's Leith crew, and importantly, was friendly with Max. "Ask him what happened last night," directed Frank. Frank listened in to the brief conversation. Max questioned, "So you're sure? Okay pal, that's great, speak soon." Upon hanging up, he responded to Frank, "Doesn't seem like anything happened in Leith boss. Damian said nothing to report." Frank scowled and paused, "Interesting, thanks for asking Max." *What the hell was Rambo talking about?*

"What's interesting? Everything okay boss?"

"No more questions over lunch Max."

"Of course, apologies."

Lunch was followed by a leisurely drive back to the capital. Bob Dylan played them home. Max could sense that Frank just wanted to chill and relax. Perhaps he was finally getting a read on his boss. As they re-entered the city, Max behaved like a model driver, adhering to all speed limits and courteously giving way to oncoming vehicles. A recovery truck driver flashed his lights in appreciation, before crawling through a tight gap between double parked cars. Frank took one look at the loaded vehicle, responding with a forced smile and a shake of the head. Max knew something was up. "You okay boss?"

"Never better son."

They pulled into Frank's drive way at 6:32pm. Max shrieked in panic, Frank appeared unmoved. Two marked police cars flanking a black BMW 3 series, presumably the unmarked car of a Detective Chief Inspector. Max had no idea how long the officers had been there, but as there were no constabulary feet on the ground, he guessed they'd not long arrived. Brazen as fuck, he pulled up behind the BMW, blocking it in. He jumped out the cabin as soon as his vehicle was stationary, the engine still running. His quick movement triggered instant reaction from every officer, six car doors opened simultaneously. Max spouted a foul mouth tirade in their general direction, "What the fuck is going on here? We've been golfing all day. You cunts got nothing better to do? Away and-" DCI Taylor silenced him mid-sentence. "Be quiet Mr Rankin, no need for deflection or distraction, I'm here for Mr Smith, not you." She walked serenely past a red-faced Max. Complete composure.

Frank remained in the passenger seat, his eyes fixated on DCI Taylor. He knew this was a time for strength, not weakness, he'd make her walk to him. A very deliberate show of power. He looked her up and down suggestively as she approached the passenger door. She confidently knocked on the window; Frank lowered it, just a touch, he knew that would annoy her. He was keen to break her focus. "Long time no see Lotte. This is quite the welcome home." He knew her, she knew him. "Fuck me, you're looking well, you been squatting?" A degrading question, deliberately condescending.

But, DCI Taylor was an experienced officer of 20 years; Frank's name didn't trouble her, his face didn't scare her, his comments didn't embarrass her. He'd been a person of interest for years but neither DCI Taylor nor her team had ever been able to prove charges. As a constable and sergeant she'd arrested tens of low level runners, with little to no impact. As an inspector; she'd tracked finance man Max for 14 months; hoping to uncover fraud, tax evasion or laundering. The investigation was eventually pulled due to insufficient evidence. As a DCI she'd gone directly after Frank, but, all his money appeared to have been cleaned, his businesses passing as legitimate. He was so smart, so elusive. That was until the night of Thursday, 26th October 2023. DCI Taylor had been presented with a golden opportunity to bring down the kingpin.

Rather than dignifying Frank's question with a response, DCI Taylor turned to her left and gave a clear instruction to her officers. "You know what folks, on second thoughts, I think Mr Rankin might have some interesting information to share with us. Yeah, I think we could pose some questions of our own down the station. Under caution of course." Maxed looked startled and like he wanted to run. He wished he hadn't gone balls deep without thinking. Turning back to Frank, DCI Taylor growled, "Right, let's skip the bravado bullshit eh Frank, you know fine well why we're here, lower your window fully." Frank obliged.

"Apologies, DCI Taylor," Frank said, innocently. "You will to have enlighten me. You see, whilst you've been chasing junkies in Pilton, I've been chasing birdies at Muirfield. Prior to that, I was in Amsterdam for six days on a pre-planned business trip."

"Well Frank, I think you've just hit a double bogey. You see, over the last six days I've been gathering and compiling some rather significant evidence. At 6pm this evening, the Procurator Fiscal sanctioned a full search of your home and vehicles. The warrant is in my car, the ink should be just about dry." The confidence in her voice unsettled Frank. He tried to keep his voice from shaking. "Fill your boots darling, no problem to me. But, if you fancied a ride in the Range Rover, you only needed to ask."

Behind Frank's suggestive wink and arrogant snigger was a brain in complete overdrive. *Dirty cunt,* he thought. *How the fuck had she produced a full search warrant on six days' notice? What evidence did she have?* He knew a number plate from Lothian Road traffic cameras wouldn't cut it. Had his many small errors morphed into an irreversible clusterfuck?

As Max was led into the back of one marked police car. Frank attempted to claw back some dominance. He figured verbally challenging the robustness of their evidence was a sensible tactic. But, before his next word could pass his lips, DCI Taylor interjected. "You know what Frank, I can just about hear the cogs turning in your head. You see, as of 3:18pm this afternoon, James Riley regained consciousness in hospital." Frank's bollocks just about crept inside him. Oh *ya cunt,* he thought. After years of laughing at the police, Frank's own shoddy workmanship had opened the door for them, and DCI Taylor was about to kick it off its hinges. He tried to keep his composure. "And who the fuck is that?" He asked, trying, but somewhat failing to sound casual.

DCI Taylor grinned, "Frank Smith, I am arresting you on suspicion of attempted murder. You do not have to say anything, but it may harm your defence if you do not mention, when questioned, something which you later rely on in court. Anything you do say may be given in evidence." Two uniformed officers assuredly stepped forward to cuff Frank, he didn't dispute, he didn't resist. A terrorising thought circulated, was he really about to experience scenario 5 in all its glory? As the car door slammed in his face, Frank felt resigned to defeat.

CHAPTER 15

BUILDING THE JIGSAW

Friday, 3rd November 2023.

It was another cold and crisp morning in the capital. The bold, smoky scent of freshly brewed coffee fragranced floor two of Police Headquarters. At 8:30am, DCI Taylor assembled her officers for the most significant team briefing of her professional life. She could sense the enthusiasm and energy within the room, it felt like a pivotal moment in time.

"Right folks, as you know, we've been looking into Frank Smith's operations for 14 long years. Let's be clear, we will never get a better opportunity to put him behind bars. I need this full process to be airtight, from start to finish." Her diligent team nodded in unison.

"Item 1. The bold Frank. Spoke to us last night with zero legal representation. Sat there like the dogs bollocks, not a care in the world. Now we know from past experience, he's a brilliant actor. It's clearly a smokescreen, nothing to hide so nothing to defend. We also know he's not a fucking idiot and we fully expect him to call upon King's Counsel at some point today. Frank claims to have returned from Amsterdam early yesterday morning. After crosschecking with border control, both flight times match his narrative and there is clear CCTV footage of him boarding and disembarking both aircrafts. He is very confident that his alibi checks out in full. He's also named two adult witnesses, who, he claims can corroborate his exact whereabouts during the timeframe in question. We hope to have both in front of us by tonight for positional statements."

"And they are?" Asked officer Maguire.

"His partner, Amber Shields and a business associate Joseph Zimmer. Replied DCI Taylor.

On the night of 26th October, Frank claims that he didn't leave his home address until around 9:45pm. Of course, we know the shooting took place sometime around 8:00pm. To that point he claims to have spent his day with close family, Amber and three-year-old son, Lucas. Clearly we need to be all over this sham, I need intel of phone data from all three parties as quickly as possible. Paterson and Devine, can you get on that immediately?" A nod from both officers. "Now we know he's lying, but, we need to be able to prove it, simple as that. I will deal with Frank directly."

DCI Taylor clicked her mouse to move on to her next slide.

"Item 2. An anonymous 999 call was received at 9:50pm on the night of the shooting. During the conversation, the individual claims to have seen a man matching Frank's description. The individual was apparently holding a handgun as he walked away from number 39. On first impression, magnificent news. The caller was even able to throw his name into the mix. Now, that might seem perfectly plausible given Frank's standing across the city. But, just consider how wet and dark that night was. How likely is it that someone fearing a gun could accurately identify an individual from across the street? Another thing for us to consider, why would it take you two hours to call the police after witnessing a shooting? Now, the reason could of course be that the shooter hung around for a period of time. But that makes zero sense to me. Or, alternatively, is someone trying to frame Frank here? Unlikely given the other items I'm about to share, but, we can't rule anything out and we have to explore every possible avenue."

DCI Taylor took a sip of coffee. "A final point on the phone call, we haven't been able to trace the mobile number. That could point towards the use of a burner, and again, potentially something more organised. We've had voice recognition teams working on the conversation, nothing concrete yet."

"Item 3. What we believe to be the money shot. Forensics have worked through the night on the Range Rover. It seemed squeaky clean until the team stumbled upon a single piece of clothing. On that piece of clothing were traces of gunshot residue. We are currently waiting on ballistics to return their match findings."

"Match findings, what do you mean boss?" Asked Paterson. DCI Taylor smiled from ear to ear, she announced confidently "Oops, I almost forgot to mention. A handgun and silencer were found at the property late last night. The bullets recovered from James' body are a perfect match. Provided our residue matches the bullets, and Frank's DNA is present on the piece of clothing, I can't see a way out for him. DNA results should be back this evening. Our search team also recovered twenty thousand pounds in cash from inside an upstairs sofa. Now that may or may not link directly to this shooting, but, it could open up other avenues and other charges."

"Ya beauty! Money shot indeed! Let's go seal the deal!" Screamed out the always effervescent officer Skinner.

"Easy tiger. Let's not get ahead of ourselves. This guy is as slippery as an eel. That's where Frank's money comes into play. Remember we are awaiting results matching the residue with the handgun. If results are deemed inconclusive in any way, that bastard Craig McCracken will rip us apart. I can picture the smug prick in court already...

"So your prosecution is based on gunshot residue, found on my clients clothing? For the benefit of the jury, my client enjoys the country lifestyle, he's been part of a shooting syndicate for the past seven years. Between the months of October and February, you will often see him holding a fired shotgun in one hand, and a brace of pheasants in the other. This trial ladies and gentlemen, is a complete waste of everyone's time and money. Mr Smith apologises unreservedly for having an unlicensed firearm in his home, he foolishly thought his shotgun license also covered that item. Should he be punished for such a mistake? Absolutely, without question. So, I'd like to make a recommendation to the court that we focus on that charge, the only factual charge in this case. Then we can then all continue with our lives having learned a very valuable lesson about gun laws and licensing. And, of course, regarding the seized cash, many a wealthy person will have a stash of money somewhere in their home. Twenty thousand pounds is proportionate and a complete non-story for a hugely successful, proven tax payer."

DCI Taylor continued. "A final, and vital point on the vehicle, folks. Following the discovery of the clothing, it would seem reasonable to assume that Frank used his personal vehicle to travel to and from the shooting. Forensics found significant tamper damage to the Range Rover's telematics control module, making the car untraceable through GPS. Clearly this creates a problem in terms of establishing his whereabouts. But, conversely, it may well point towards further criminal activity on Frank's part. Tampering alone makes the vehicle instantly uninsurable and therefore illegal. My next thought was then a simple one, let's just trawl Lothian Road surveillance, that should bookend the incident perfectly. But, the tsunami like weather on the evening of the 26th makes it impossible to identify any vehicle models or number plates travelling north or south."

"So everything rests on ballistics and DNA then boss?" Asked Devine.

"Yes and no," replied DCI Taylor.

"Item 4. Frank's partner of seven years Amber, was not at the property yesterday evening. Apparently she is out of town with her son Lucas, due to return at lunchtime today. Is that a coincidence? Maybe aye, maybe no. According to Frank, she's been in Aberdeen the last week, spending time with her friend Steph. Again, we need to verify that. Let's find her, and speak with her immediately."

"You think they might be in cahoots?" Questioned officer McMullan.

"Don't know. What I will say is, Frank's a master manipulator. I wouldn't discount any possible scenario." A voice from the back of the room piped up. "Is Lucas Frank's boy?"

"What makes you ask that officer Thom?" Responded an intrigued DCI Taylor.

"Just exploring all avenues, boss."

"Yes. So, we think Frank and Amber's relationship began sometime in 2015. Lucas was born 21st June 2020. Frank and Amber have lived at their current address since late 2016. However, you raise a very good point. I want a deep dive on the status of their relationship. A man like him can't be easy to live with, never mind raise a child with. I'm convinced Amber will give up information regarding their interactions, good or bad. Skinner and McMullan that's you two."

DCI Taylor clicked onto her last slide.

"Item 5. Finally, finally, finally. The key player in all this remains the victim, Mr James Riley. Other than our anonymous caller, no one else saw or heard a thing that night. As soon as he is able, I need a full statement of events. A positive ID destroys Frank and any nonsense alibi. His son Charlie is only five, and understandably won't talk about the shooting. He has been through significant trauma. His mother died back in 2018, he was just a few months old. He's just witnessed the attempted murder of his father. Now, we all know Frank's reputation, James cannot be hushed into silence. If Frank was the man who shot him, we have to get every detail out of him. At the risk of repeating myself for a hundredth time, we cannot fail, we owe it to James and Charlie. Thom and Maguire, I need you checking on the condition of James periodically. As soon as he can speak, you are the first two faces he sees. Right, let's go to work team."

Officers Paterson and Devine interviewed Joseph Zimmer at 10:15am. He was confident and assured throughout the process, calmly detailing his late night meeting with Frank. He was happy to share all text and email correspondence between the pair, interactions that spanned many years. Without hesitation he disclosed that Frank had contacted him to postpone their meeting by 30 minutes.

"Are 10:00pm meetings common practice between yourself and Mr Smith?" Inquired Devine.

"Yes they are, have been for ten years. Feel free to check my diary entries too. Frank and I have been close for a very long time. Our meetings are as much a friendly catch-up as they are a business discussion."

"And what was the reason given for postponing Mr Zimmer?

"His little boy was restless at bedtime. Frank is a complex guy, you're never quite sure what he's thinking most of the time. But, one thing is for sure, his priorities have changed in recent years. He'd drop anything for Lucas, he's the single most precious thing in his life now."

"You say Mr Smith's priorities have changed, what did he prioritise prior to Lucas?"

"Oh, he was just focused on business, you know. Nothing and no one took him away from profitability and financial success."

"And what was his demeanour like when you met that night?" Asked Paterson.

"Just the same old Frank; captivating, funny, strategic. We discussed property and fund management for maybe 40 minutes and then we spoke about family and holidays for half an hour or so. He didn't stay long, he had an early flight to catch."

The interview lasted 50 minutes in all. It was a fluid and seemingly transparent conversation from start to finish.

Skinner and McMullan picked up Amber at 2:17pm. Gayle agreed to babysit, the thought of her daughter being involved in a police incident made her nauseous. Amber started the interview by

stating, "I'm really not sure how much help I'll be, but I'll certainly do what I can to support your line of inquiry." A brazen Skinner shouted, jumping from his seat, slamming both hands on the table. "Listen blondie, this isn't basic fucking instinct. A flash of the fanny doesn't help you here." He sat back down and smirked. "Even though it might help me, haha." Amber gave a repulsed looked, then smiled sarcastically, turning her head 45 degrees. "Officer McMullan, can you please pop a muzzle on your colleague."
He replied with a giggle, "Right let's get into this eh?"

The interview lasted a mere 30 minutes. Closing remarks came from Skinner, "Thanks darling, that was lovely, you're now free to go."

Craig McCracken arrived to meet Frank at 4:00pm. Frank was understandably panicked and irritable. "The cunt's woke up Craig! He's fucking woke up!"

"Relax Frank", replied the lawyer serenely. This is a game of cat and mouse. Now, I don't have a clue what official documentation is about to land on my desk but I can assure you, it isn't a victim statement from James. I've done my background checks. It's a miracle that he survived. Is he conscious? Yes. Is he able to speak or communicate effectively? Absolutely not. Waking up hasn't necessarily improved his chances of recovery, or his ability to testify against you in court. He has suffered a life threatening pneumothorax. Essentially, his right lung has completely collapsed due to significant gunshot trauma. His only focus right now is trying to breathe and survive. He's still being heavily supported by a ventilator, he's unable to talk or communicate in any way, and he won't walk for a number of weeks, if ever again. My advice to you? Try to get some rest over the weekend. I'll know everything I need to know by tomorrow evening, then we attack this thing head on

Monday morning. Sound good?" Frank took a deep breath and nodded. "Yeah, sounds great. Thanks."

CHAPTER 16

PILLS AND THRILLS

Spring 2019.

Carol and Martin knew they would have to take an active role in James' mourning and recovery. Coaxed by Carol, Martin had encouraged James to join him for dinner, play a round of golf, sink a few beers, even just sit silently in the cinema. He'd maybe asked a dozen times in the six months immediately following Rachel's death. James had always been a great socialiser; larger than life, a brilliant listener, a hilarious drunk. But losing Rachel had gutted him beyond recovery it seemed. When asked about availability, James had a pre-rehearsed list of excuses; "I can't get a babysitter, I've got work to catch up on, Charlie has a cold, money is a bit tight, maybe next weekend mate."

Carol and Martin knew all the signs. Unsurprisingly, James had been diagnosed with clinical depression, nine weeks after Rachel's death. A diagnosis was only possible because of Carol's persistent pressure and unwavering support. James was immediately medicated; prescribed Sertraline; 50mgs a day, increased through request and review, up to a maximum of 200mgs a day. Getting out of bed, brushing his teeth, taking a shower, drinking fluids; simple, everyday tasks had become Everest like to James. Throughout his mourning process, he continued to deliberately isolate himself; the thought of doing something, anything, particularly in public, was all too much.

Martin was very aware of how insular and solitary James' behaviour had become, only leaving the house to take Charlie on a single midday walk. When James did leave the house, he looked a shadow of his former self; dishevelled, unshaven and exhausted.

All food shops were delivered to the house; as were all presents, gifts, toys, clothes etc. He was simply existing as a housebound hermit; a worrying thought considering he had full custody and complete responsibility over baby Charlie. Carol wanted to intervene as legal Guardian, but, was fully aware that a balance had to be struck between nurture and privacy. The last thing she wanted was to offend, and create more distance and isolation.

Carol began subtly dropping in with Jeff on a Wednesday evening, she wasn't too sure what she would find or observe. As time passed, James slowly began to enjoy the adult company, and Charlie smiled and giggled every time he saw big gentle Jeff. Neglect or squalor? Nothing could be further from the truth. Whilst James himself appeared to be falling apart, he was doing everything he could for his boy. Charlie was loved, supported and nourished. Although it seemed James had forgotten how to survive as an individual, he was clearly able to provide and care for Charlie. It was almost as if he was sacrificing his own life for that of his son.

Spring time seemed to offer some perspective and positivity. James wasn't sure if increased sunlight played a part, possibly the rising temperature, maybe a combination of both. By May 2019, he had stabilised on his medication; Sertaline had been replaced by Citalopram, 40mgs daily allowed him to function to a satisfactory level. With his mindset seemingly improving, Carol mooted the proposal to Martin, that she could perhaps stay with James for a night or two during the week to give him some much needed down time. Martin rubbished the notion, claiming it to be "Fucking weird" and "Too close to home."

"Right, well you need to bloody step up then darling," challenged Carol. "The poor guy and little Charlie need us." Martin agreed, but had clear boundaries as a loving and protective husband.

Martin yet again asked about availability, this time, for a football match, Hibernian vs Aberdeen. He had a spare ticket as Sarah had made plans with friends. Growing up, James had been a good player. He had represented Hibs from age 12 to age 19. He even graduated to the first team squad, a one time substitute appearance in the Scottish League Cup in 2004. Thereafter, he focused on his more realistic professional career, but continued to play in the Scottish Highland League whilst completing his architecture degree.

Before marrying Rachel, and having Charlie, he enjoyed returning to Easter Road and watching his team. The match day atmosphere was so special, 15,000 home fans passionately belting out Sunshine on Leith could reduce any mere mortal to tears. Pre-match was always filled with uncertainty, regardless of who the opposition were or what the competition was. The actual match itself was usually immersive; but on occasion, could be utter pish. The post-match was either filled with excitement or misery. That's been the life of every Hibs supporter over the clubs' near 150 year history. But, that forms part of the magic; the highs are so euphoric, and the lows are so dismal. Unlike every other time, James didn't say no to Martin. He requested some think time, then, two days later he asked Carol to watch Charlie for an hour so he could get a haircut. James was about to exit his self-imposed seven month exile from society.

James agreed to go to the match for one reason. He wanted to see if he could feel again. Whenever he held Charlie, he felt all the love and emotion a father should. However, everything else he used to enjoy in life had slowly drifted, to the point of complete numbness. He'd lost interest in everything that once made him smile; work, football, socialising, working out. He wondered if the Easter Road crowd and Premiership matchday experience could rekindle a sense of drive and passion within him.

The match was the final league fixture of the 2018-2019 season. Tickets were easy to come by; the game was a dead rubber for Hibs, they had already secured 5th position, one place ahead of their arch rivals, Hearts. Aberdeen were in 4th place but couldn't be caught. For Aberdeen, the match was a massive opportunity, they had the chance to catch Kilmarnock in 3rd place. As the morning of the match arrived, James did indeed begin to feel nervous. Nothing to do with the football though, it was the thought of drinking whilst on Citalopram. He knew he'd need to have a couple of beers in order to relax and loosen up, but not knowing how the chemicals would mix made him very uneasy.

Martin picked James up at 11:30am on Sunday 19th May. He was pleasantly surprised with how James looked and presented. He seemed bubbly when he sat in the passenger's seat and was genuinely grateful that Martin had invited him. James was dressed in a cosy duck down, knee length puffer jacket. Underneath he wore a smart black polo shirt, slim fit back jeans and black high-top trainers, Wrapped around his neck, a green 1980s Hibernian FC scarf, gifted to him by his estranged father. After some general chitchat and football based banter, James questioned, "Early start this sir?"

"Last game of the season old boy! Few beers pre-match, then into the stadium to soak up the atmosphere, followed by gins up the town post-match. Magic!"

"No no," I'll need to get back for the youngster."

"Negative!" Replied a blunt, excited Martin. "We're out for the night shagger, and you're staying at mine, it's a bank holiday tomorrow! Carol has got Charlie and will stay at yours."

"Mmm, I don't know mate. Can we see how things go? I'm conscious of drinking on these fucking tablets", an unsure response, from a cagey James. They both looked at each other and smiled.

The match kicked off, Hibs started brightly. Wingers, Murray and Horgan, and attacking midfielder, Mallan all forcing excellent saves from the Aberdeen goalkeeper, Cerny. Pressure continued to build throughout the first half but Aberdeen were always dangerous on the counterattack, particularly the industrious midfield duo of Shinnie and Ferguson, and powerhouse striker

Cosgrove. Hibs deservingly took the lead in the 26th minute, McNulty finishing expertly after being put through on goal by Murray. Murray then whipped an effort past the right post, a chance he really should have converted. On 43 minutes, Hibs were punished for their inefficiency in front of goal. McLennan beat Gray 1 vs. 1 on the left wing, his cut back was met by the onrushing Cosgrove, who finished coolly left footed beyond Marciano. An entertaining half of football, and a typical Hibs performance, dominant but drawing. Martin was delighted with how responsive James was to the action on the pitch, he seemed to be enjoying it, he was emotionally invested, he was smiling again.

The second half was a different affair. Horgan's left-footed curling effort almost restored the lead. But from there, the home teams defensive frailties were laid bare. James turned to Martin, "It's the old classic, you have to score when you're on top against good opposition." As Aberdeen cranked up the pressure, Hibs began to creak like a sinking ship. Four second half bookings exposed their poor discipline, and highlighted how weak and ragged they could become. Aberdeen dominated possession and created many more chances, deservedly taking the lead in the 63rd minute, May setting up Wilson for a simple finish. So, a 2-1 home defeat, bowing out of season 2018-19 with a fucking whimper, typical Hibs.

Aberdeen supporters jubilantly celebrated at the final whistle, knowing they'd snatched 3rd place. But, to their dismay, word began to filter through to the capital that Kilmarnock had beaten Rangers 2-1 at Rugby Park thanks to a last minute Brophy winner, snatching 3rd place back. This news was music to the ears of the Easter Road faithful. The Hibs fans laughed and jeered for two reasons; the Aberdeen fans were devastated at missing out on a Europa League playoff place, and, the highly rated Steve Clarke would soon be departing Kilmarnock to become the Scotland manager. Football, the most fickle of sports.

After some deliberations, James eventually agreed to join Martin up the town for some 'end of season drinks.' James remained apprehensive, he was definitely more drunk than he should have been after four pints of lager, a bovril and a scotch pie. "We just jumping into a few footy boozers aye?"

"No, no!" Declared a merry Martin.

"Two lads from work, Norrie and Dave, have sorted a booth up George Street. I've also booked us a table at a club for later. I asked them if a big sexy hunk could join us."

"Ah, okay," responded a now cynical James. *This prick is trying to get me wrecked,* he thought. But, as James relaxed over several gin and tonics, he began to enjoy the interactions with Martin and his rather eccentric colleagues. Both were warm and witty, their humour mischievous and suggestive. On first impression, Norrie was a genuine loose cannon who only had two settings, loud and louder. A sex mad, hyperactive Physical Education teacher, who James figured must have been on the radar of the General Teaching Council. Whilst his comedic timing was exemplary, all he spoke about the full night was women and shagging.

The other was deadpan Science teacher, Dave. A recent divorcee after 'accidentally riding' a fellow scientist at his schools Christmas party. The stupid bastard had left his phone unsupervised after falling asleep on the en-suite toilet. His heartbroken wife discovering cringeworthy, suggestive texts as he lay snoring.

"There's clearly chemistry between us, might as well be on my fucking gravestone," a staring, monotone Dave murmured. Martin and Norrie burst out laughing simultaneously. James was less enamoured with the messages, he'd give anything to have his wife back.

Things got more awkward as the brazen Norrie interjected. "Hey, Martin, Carol no binned you yet? What a fucking honey she is." Martin and James glanced at each other awkwardly and took a sobering sip. "All good thanks pal." A very quick change of subject from Dave, "right lads, drink up, time for a dance."

At 12:50am, the group queued outside CC Blooms, on Calton Square. A now befuddled Norrie, projected like a foghorn, "This place no for gays?" Dave hurriedly shushed him, "Norrie, lower your fucking voice." Martin growled, "You'd rather be called a gay than a paedo, no? This is the only club in town where over 30's are actively welcomed. And the tunes are fucking excellent. Relax man, enjoy."

"As long as we're banging by the end of the night! And, when I say banging, a mean birds, no each other."

"Yes, thanks for clarifying," Dave responded sarcastically. A friendly doorman opened the main entrance, Frankie Goes to Hollywood enticed them towards the dance floor. The atmosphere was electric, the beat from Two Tribes could turn any cool cat walk into an impromptu hip thrusting dance-off. Norrie flung himself over Dave, crudely screaming in his left ear, "Fancy a couple of keys sir? Got some minted gear on me."

"Abso-fucking-lutely," replied Dave.

At the bar, Martin ordered eight tequilas and four bottles of Peroni. James had already resigned himself to a hellish Sunday. He thought to himself, *might as well just fucking go for it.* After double tequilas, the foursome took to the floor, beer in hand. Madonna's Vogue turned the place into a finger clicking sass fest.

Iconic songs continued to play, many more shots were downed. After a time, James started to feel a little nauseous. He wasn't used to the sheer volume of alcohol that was being consumed. He headed to the downstairs toilet for a tactical pitstop. Norrie immediately followed him. "Right shagger, give your face a slash of water and get a sniff at this, you'll be squared up in no time."

"Na, I'm good Norrie pal, I'm already on hunners eh drugs coz of Rachel."

"Well then, what harm is one more gonna do? Hahahaha, come on you."

"Right, fuck it, moan then." Peer pressure, man's biggest weakness. James snorted two big bumps off Norrie's car key. They returned to the dance floor, Martin and Dave had creeped to the very back of the club, where it was near pitch black, 400 fluid silhouettes rocking out to Billy Idol's White Wedding. James felt sharper again, more alert, more awake. But, definitely needed some water to wash down the sickly sweet taste of tequila. He thanked a barman for his drink and turned to his right, attempting to hide the bottle, afraid he would be branded a lightweight shandy bastard from the prancing trio.

As he drank from the bottle, James heard a feminine scream from behind, "No fucking way! James Riley! How the hell are you? You hunky devil." James turned around and was immediately entranced by her beauty, it was the insatiable Amber. She was older, obviously, but instantly recognisable, instantly exciting. "Wow! Amber. Hi. How are you? You look, eh, incredible, wow! How long's it been?"

"Oh gees, I don't know James, eight or nine years I guess."

"That's right! Summer 2011! How could I forget." Both felt an immediate connection. They stared intently into each others eyes. James didn't want to feel it, he really didn't, but this woman seemed magnetic. Amber smiled, "well then, are you gonna hug me or not?" Physical contact confirmed their chemistry was stronger than ever. Both knew the evening was about to get very interesting.

James bought them both a gin and tonic. "So who you out with then," asked Amber. "Oh, just a few friends. Well, in actual fact, my neighbour and a couple of lads I've never met before. They're fucking mad with it though, I'd sneaked away for some water when you called on me. What about you?" A flirty Amber responded, "I'm out with a few girlfriends, but they're away dancing their asses off, I fancied a bit more of a chilled one. You know, an early night." James responded, "A chilled one? Is that still the case?" Biting her bottom lip, a fascinated Amber replied, "Na, I've had a change of heart, looks like business is about to pick up. Fancy getting a taxi somewhere Mr Riley?"

"Eh, yeah, sure. I do, I definitely do. Can we go to your place?" Amber winked, "Course darling, you hosted the last time. Just let me nip to the bathroom. Oh, and I'll let the girls know I'm calling it a night."

CHAPTER 17

ARCHITECT OF HIS OWN DOWNFALL

James and Amber jumped in the first black cab they could see after leaving the club. Once the fresh Edinburgh air hit James, he couldn't see much at all. As red lights indicated secured doors, James' conscience made a brief appearance. But it stood no chance versus the excitement and arousal levels of the current situation. A sharp intake of breath from Amber, "Fuck!" James replied instantly, "What's up? You okay?"

"I've left something in CCs."

"What is it? Your phone? Your bag?" Amber's face filled with mischief and lust. "My knickers."

The pair laughed uncontrollably. Amber eventually breaking the hilarity by pouncing onto James' lap. She straddled him for the duration of the seven minute journey. The driver couldn't drive quick enough along Queen Street, he felt like a nerve-racked intern photographer, experiencing his first day on a porno set. An emergency stop outside Amber's house brought an immediate halt to the kissing, biting and licking. Amber was catapulted forward, landing firming on her arse. "Fuck sake driver, any need for that?" Shouted James.

"Pay the fare and get to fuck, couple of horny bastards." James threw him a twenty pound note. "Keep the change pal, fucking idiot."

The pair held hands as they walked to Amber's front door. "Bloody hell Amber! That's some pad, and a brand new Range Rover to match!"

"That's what happens when you stick in at medical school Jamesy boy."

"Wow! Speaking of wow, how's the ass?"

Amber giggled, "nicely warmed up, ready for a proper spanking." She turned the key, then firmly pushed the door open. Almost simultaneously, she grabbed James by the shirt and slammed him against the wall, cracking a floor to ceiling hall mirror in the process. As they kissed passionately, Amber wanted to assert her authority this time round, ripping his shirt wide open, scattering buttons onto the tiled floor. Placing her right index finger on his lips, she instructed, "Go to the fridge and get yourself a bottle of water. I want you at your very best big boy, no semi-final flops." James sniggered, "You needn't worry about that! Amber smiled, turned and walked towards the front door. "Where you off to?" Asked James.

"I'll be five minutes, just going to grab a condom."

"A condom? Changed days!"

"You see a lot of nasty things as a doctor. Can't be too cautious, you handsome types always have big body counts." James struggled to laugh at that final comment, thoughts of Rachel flooded his mind once again.

He sat at the marble breakfast bar, each swig of water seemed to sober him a touch. On his final gulp, Amber re-entered the room, dressed in a lipstick red satin rope, open at front, not a stitch of underwear on. "Wow," James declared. He thought, *this thing is perfection; alopecia from the eyebrows down, midget gem nipples, six pack abs, hourglass hips, long athletic legs. God himself couldn't back out of this situation.*

Amber's bedside alarm clock clicked past 3:00am. The pair lay on their backs, panting like spent border collies after an epic day on the farm. Beads of warm sweat dripped from their toned bodies onto already soaked sheets. Amber turned and placed her head on James' chest, her right hand on his stomach. She could hear his heart racing, she enjoyed listening to it during a moment of prolonged, yet comfortable silence. "Well that was fucking incredible," stated James.

"Wasn't it just." Amber kissed his chest and removed the condom. As she grabbed her robe, half a dozen wrappers fell on the floor. "Fuck me! We going again!?" Asked a surprised James. Amber laughed, "Don't panic! Fingers like cows teats me! Had them in my glove compartment and somehow managed to burst the entire packet trying to get one out! Just nipping down stairs, won't be long."

James simply lay there, smiling about how brilliantly random his day had been. *Condoms in your car? How fucking bizarre, he* thought. With the perfect blend of alcohol and euphoria flowing through his body, James' mind wandered off into an augmented reality. He began to analyse a homemade case study, comparing the atrocious Hibs performance of twelve hours before, to that of the magnificent Amber. Amber was hungrier, she was better conditioned, she was willing to do the dirty work, she loved a hard tackle, she was composed under pressure, she made home advantage count. And, perhaps most importantly, she demanded standards from those around her. If only Hibs had half of her attributes and qualities, they'd have a fighting chance of qualifying for Europe!

Clattering and clinking from downstairs returned James to the softly lit luxurious bedroom. Another humorous thought entered his mind. *What the fucks she doing down there? Making a protein shake with my junk?* A few minutes later, Amber returned, holding two perfectly garnished Tanqueray and tonics. Amber flaunted her stunning body as he walked across the room and passed James his chilled drink.

"Cheers sir."

"Where the hell you been? That was an age," inquired James.

"Quality takes time babe, enjoy." Amber winked and smiled.

"I just love your confidence Amber. Your self-assuredness, it's very sexy."

"Haha. Don't be fooled, I only feel like that when you're around."
"What?" Replied a confused, pausing James.
"Haha. Kidding on pal! Cheers."
The pair finished their drinks. Then hugged, kissed and chatted, until Amber eventually feel asleep in James' arms. Conversation had flowed easily, but, both could sense the other was holding back information.

James woke just after 8am, an admiring Amber stared and smiled as she stroked his chest. The glint in her emerald green eyes suggested one simple thing, love. Morning sunlight further emphasised her natural beauty. James smiled back and said, "Good morning," but, his dark, sunken eyes told a different story. His throat was dry, his head pounding, his stomach churning. Whilst Amber looked to be planning round two, James' peaky expression suggested he'd rather jump out the nearest window than resume fornication. The overriding emotion was shame. His first night out drinking and he'd managed to bed someone. And, not a random someone at that, an old flame from eight years ago, who, looked like a fucking movie star, and seemed to have the personality to match.

Amber's keenness concerned James. Thanks to drink and drugs, she'd seen his best fake smile in its truest form. The harsh reality was that he was still emotionally wrecked; riddled by depression and trauma. He only had love for Charlie now, there simply wasn't room for someone else in his life.

As Amber continued to chat, James' spinning mind wandered, focusing on his lavish surroundings. He questioned internally... Was Amber really who she claimed to be? She'd clearly been successful in life, but, this was no 28-year-old doctors house.
Was she a liar?
Did she have a man?
And, if so, what the fuck was he?
A gangster? An investment banker? A footballer?
Something just didn't add up.

Amber offered James a shower, he declined abruptly.

"No I'm okay, I'll just grab a glass of water."

"You tinky bastard," joked Amber. "Well, I'm going for one. Nip downstairs and help yourself. There's water, juice and milk in the fridge."

James spent the next five minutes nervously searching Amber's home. He scanned for family photographs and couples signage as he walked downstairs. He sneaked to the front door to check for slippers or shoes, then hurriedly jogged to the back door to see if he could find any man sized coats or jackets. Then a quick gander in the fridge for any beers or ciders. Finally, he checked for a house phone, perhaps the answering machine would give her away? Nope! Nothing to be seen or heard, literally. Apart for a very impressive selection of artwork scattered throughout the house, everything else seemed so orderly and characterless. Perhaps Amber was indeed a singleton. Maybe everything was legitimate after all.

A jubilant Amber, dressed in a figure hugging tracksuit skipped downstairs to meet James in the kitchen. "You want a lift home pal?" Asked Amber.

"Would that be okay? I need to get back to my wee boy. My neighbour, Carol is looking after him."

"Ah, yes, of course. Beautiful Charlie."

"Charlie, how'd you know Charlie?"

"Haha! You really were pissed last night! You spoke about him for ages over that last glass of gin. You showed me hundreds of pictures, remember? It was very cute Mr Riley." James couldn't recall anything of that conversation, but recognised that he was a little worse for wear and had just been ridden like a grand national winner for the best part of an hour.

Amber drove south on Lothian Road, the time was 8:49am. Bank Holiday morning traffic was light as expected. James directed her to Bramble Place. "What's the number again?" Asked Amber.

"Eh, well, I live at 39, but drop me at 51 please. I was meant to be staying with Martin last night." Amber smiled, then indicated and pulled into a free space outside number 51. "A lads tale, always stick to the original story eh!" A now awkward James said, "Right well, thanks so much. That was a fun night. Maybe see you around." His left hand reaching for the door handle.

Amber's left hand grabbed onto his right wrist. "Wait a fucking minute! Come on James, can I at least get your number? A peck on the cheek?" James paused nervously. "No, I'm afraid not Amber. It's really complicated. I wish things were different, but they aren't."

"Okay darling, well, how about I give you my number and if things change, you can call me?"

Her warm smile settled James again. "Yeah, sure. That sounds good." As soon as he clicked saved, James leaned over, kissed Amber on the cheek, then exited the vehicle.

He walked into number 51, the front door was ajar. A quick glance into the living room confirmed that Martin had got home safely. He lay fully clothed, sound asleep on the brown leather sofa, a half eaten doner kebab balancing on his lap. A tail wagging Jeff sat at the top of the stairs. James headed straight upstairs to the spare room. It was time to rest his head and body without fear, Jeff jumped up and cuddled into his feet at the base of the bed. James thought about dropping Amber a quick message, but, after another scrambled thought, decided it was best not to. Amber took a minute to text a couple of friends, then picked a playlist, before pulling away in the Range Rover. She had a busy few hours ahead of her.

CHAPTER 18

CHANGE THE NARRATIVE

Saturday, 11th November 2023.

Rambo knew he had to speak with Frank. He arranged a one-to-one visit at the earliest opportunity. His drive to Saughton Prison was made in silence, a hundred Frank reactions ruminating in his head. Apprehension was a completely new feeling for Rambo. Until this moment he'd always been transparent, no need to worry, no need to explain. He wondered how he could seek forgiveness from the one man he truly loved and respected. Rambo was the first visitor to enter the large magnolia painted hall at 1:01pm. It comprised of a central walkway, flanked by facing rows and circular pods of maybe 100 navy blue seats. Natural light shone through barred and frosted clerestory windows. A strong smell of disinfectant completed the clinical feel. Rambo scanned as he walked, looking for his boss and friend.

Frank sat isolated and alone towards the back of the room, his head bowed, a hand placed on each knee. "Frank!" Shouted Rambo. An unkempt Frank didn't move an inch, he didn't respond in any way.

Patrolling guards and blinking CCTV units made it difficult for anyone to relax and enjoy reunion or conversation. Rambo sat opposite Frank, awkwardly rubbing his bosses upper arm in a nervous attempt to comfort him. "Hi Frank, how you doing?" Zero interaction from Frank, nothing. "Boss, it's Rambo, you eh, you okay?" Not even the shrug of a shoulder, or a simple hand gesture in acknowledgment.

Frank's statue still presentation worried Rambo. He immediately catastrophised about possible causes.

Had Frank been consumed by depression?
Had the bastards medically sedated him?
Or worse, had he been lobotomised?
All made up nonsense.

"Listen, Frank-" Just that second Frank raised his head, exposing irritated, darkened eyes, his hands gripping tightly into trouser fabric. An immediate challenge question, "John, what have you done?" Rambo tried to speak but was cut off immediately.
"What the fuck have you done? You've fucked me, you've ended me." For maybe the first time in his life, Rambo released some physical emotion of his own, his voice cracking in response.
"Frank I'm sorry. I'm so sorry. I had to do it."
Frank's sleep deprived eyes filled with tears, he responded through gritted teeth. "But why Rambo? I've done nothing but help you, protect you, your whole fucking life, and this is how you repay me?"

"All I can say is sorry. What was I supposed to do Frank? She's family." Frank screwed up his face in confusion. "What the fuck you talking about?"

Both men sat in silence, eyes locked on one another. It seemed the weakest would blink first. Rambo gave a smirk. "You don't even know what I'm apologising for do you?"

"Rambo, I'm no in the mood for fucking games. If I'm getting mind raped by a simpleton like you, it really is time to throw in the fucking towel." Rambo's smirk turned to a laugh. Frank's confusion had returned him to a position of comfort and composure. His trademark cyborg stare returned. "I lied about Leith Frank, I was in Pilton sorting out a family issue, I had to act, I couldn't let it slide. I know I should have said but I didn't want to trouble you, it was personal."

"What sort of family issue?" Questioned a now interested Frank. Rambo faltered. "It's eh, it's fucking Tina. She's back on the skag. She's gonna end up losing Jamie again, for good this time, that'll kill her before any drugs do. She was doing okay but there's so much new gear getting punted the now, it's fucking everywhere, it's impossible to avoid."

Frank paused briefly, then responded. "Right, so you acted? Everything's sorted? No disrespect Rambo, but I couldn't give a fuck about your sister, Tina was lost as a teenager." The comment rocked Rambo. "How can you say that Frank? Your Michael died at 16. You'd never describe him as lost." Frank snapped, "Don't you ever mention my brother's name again, you fucking hear me?" Rambo apologised immediately. "I'm sorry, that was uncalled for." Once emotions had settled, Frank reinstalled some focus. "Right, can we prioritise me now, and this cunt of a situation you've put me in?"
Rambo interjected. "Yeah, course boss, but, first I need your advice."

"Do you aye?" Questioned Frank sarcastically.

"Yeah. You see, I went a bit guerrilla, some intimidation tactics. You know. The dealer I taught a lesson to was a lad called Robbie Rivera." Frank puffed his cheeks, a change of tone, "Robbie Rivera? You big rough cunt Rambo. What you do to him? You do know who his father is?" Rambo responded, "I know who his father is now yeah. I presumed he was a low level idiot, I thought it was a chance to send a clear message. I took two of his fingers." Frank almost choked. "You chopped his fingers off? Holy fuck man."

"Well, a thumb and a finger." You'll sort it eh Frank? I mean, I'm untouchable, protected. You know?" Frank laughed, mocking Rambo. "You fucking moron. You're untouchable because I make it so. If I get sent down you're fair game. You know what, you might just be a dead man walking Rambo. The last guy who crossed Roberto Rivera ended up in a deep fat fryer."

"No cunts taking me out." Replied a defiant Rambo. A disappointed Frank pointed at his chest, specifically his heart. "You see, this is why I'm the fucking boss, this is why I make the decisions. I don't let emotions get in the way of business." Recent events made it difficult for Frank to believe his own words, but, as always his delivery brought credibility.

The heated conversation had attracted interest from circulating guards. Three had congregated for a chat, all peering in the general direction of Frank and Rambo. After they'd dispersed, Frank scanned the area for any other prying eyes and ears. He lowered his voice to a near whisper and leaned forward. "Listen Rambo, you have two options here. You either take your medicine and accept whatever punishment is coming your way, and it's fucking coming by the way, Roberto will pick his moment to strike. Or, you take control, you change the narrative." Rambo nodded his head, Frank had provided him with instant clarity.

Just then, Frank grabbed Rambo by both shoulders. "Good luck. Now let's get on to the main fucking course shall we?" Frank stared into Rambo's eyes like a prize fighter at weigh-in, he scanned for weakness and deception. "A man's eyes speak louder than his words, you know that better than most John."

After prolonged discussion, Rambo left Saughton Prison at 1:57pm. Frank was returned to his cell to reflect and contemplate, before the arrival of Amber at 3:00pm.

Just as Rambo had done two hours previous, Amber scanned the visitors hall for Frank. As soon as they locked eyes, she removed her aviator style sunglasses. As always, Amber looked stunning, she wore a dark grey double breasted blazer and dark grey flannel straight leg trousers. Frank's slovenly appearance shocked her, his usual tailored suit replaced by baggy tracksuit bottoms and an oversized, ill-fitting t-shirt.

A mere 96 hours had ticked by since he'd been formally charged with attempted murder, but the stress and pressure of the whole process had haggard his face. Amber wasn't sure how she'd be received, the couple hadn't spoke since the night of the shooting, some 16 days before.

"Amber!" Frank welcomed his partner with open arms. Amber smiled, her nerves immediately settled. The couple embraced for several seconds, Amber's arms wrapped tightly around Frank's waist. Frank gently kissed her forehead, his right hand supporting the back of her head. He ran his fingers through her thick blonde hair, a further sign of affection and closeness. They sat simultaneously, Amber wiping away tears with a tissue. "Frank I'm so sorry. You don't deserve this, you were only protecting me."

Frank scanned the room tentatively, signalling to Amber to lower her voice. He replied softly in a calm voice, "Amber, please, I don't need any apologies from you. It's done. You know I'd do anything for you and Lucas. I don't regret it, not for a second. How is he? How is the wee man?" Amber offered her right hand, Frank kissed it then held and caressed it in a tender grasp. "He's doing great Frank. He's asking for you. I just keep saying daddy's away on a business trip. That has pacified him for now." Frank's eyes began to fill up with tears, "Well you tell him daddy loves him and that he's the best boy." Amber bubbled and nodded her head. "What happens if you're found guilty Frank? We can't function without you."

"Shh shh shh. Amber you have my word, regardless of what happens to me, you'll be taken care of, I promise." Amber smiled through streaming tears, her bottom lip quivering uncontrollably. "What's the process from here?" Asked Amber.

Frank listed likely timescales and outcomes. It seemed the case could last for months and months. "I'm in constant dialogue with Craig. He has all the information he needs now and is looking into every option. He seems confident."

"He always is," replied a whispering Amber.

"When I know more, you'll hear. The key thing for you is to not to say a word, nothing. This whole thing remains our secret, is that clear?" Amber struggled to keep her emotions in check, "Yeah, very clear, 100%, our secret."

Frank reassured her again, "Come here babe. I need you to be strong, for me, for Lucas." Amber wiped away more tears. The couple hugged for a final time, Amber then turned and walked towards the exit. Frank stared and smiled as she left the room.

Sunday, 12th November 2023. Roberto Rivera locked up Rivera's Fish and Chip shop on West Granton Road, the time was 11:10pm. Whilst the shop acted as a front for his heroin empire, it was a reputable business in its own right, serving the residents of Granton and Pilton for over 20 years. Roberto's immaculate appearance just screamed Italian gangster; slick back black hair, three piece suit, knee length woollen overcoat. He hadn't battered a piece of haddock since 2005, but still visited the shop every Sunday to tally up the weeks legal and illegal takings.

As he dropped the final graffiti covered shutter, he felt a sudden pressure in his lower back. Roberto clenched both fists out of frustration, "Fuck," he whispered. "Turnaround and walk to my pickup." Instructed an armed Rambo. An unprepared Roberto replied, "Ah, Rambo. I was hoping to catch up with you this week."

"Don't I fucking know it. No time like the present eh?" Rambo poked and prodded Roberto in the ribs with the firearm as they approached the Ford Ranger." Roberto pleaded, "Listen big man, it's me who should be upset with you, no? You walking into my patch is ballsy, I'll give you that. Can we just drop this, call it even and move on?"

"Robbie being your son has fuck all to do with me. Putting your own blood in harms way is your doing, not mine." Roberto wanted to respond smartly, but recognised the perilous situation he found himself in. Rambo was angry and feared no man. Roberto was ordered to sit in the drivers seat, Rambo sat directly behind him, wedging the gun barrel between the headrest and squab.
The engine was still running. Rambo instructed, "Drive to Leith Docks, I'll direct from there."

The pickup drove straight into a derelict factory shed. "Stop the engine and get out." Instructed Rambo. Roberto knew he had to do something, and quick. He stupidly decided that his best form of defence was attack. He turned to face Rambo and laughed. "Do you have any idea who you are messing with here? You've just signed your own suicide note, big doss cunt."

From nowhere, Rambo hit Roberto with an overhand right, cracking his jaw on impact. Roberto folded like a deck chair, the back of his head smacking off the oily concrete floor as he fell. He tried desperately to get back to his feet but had the concussive motor skills of a newly born giraffe. Rambo kicked him with all his might, once to the abdomen, once to the face. Roberto lay there bloodied and coughing, able to hear, unable to move or speak. His immediately swollen eyes lost all focus, only able to make out faint movement in the near distance. Rambo disappeared into darkness then returned maybe 30 seconds later, carrying an old teak chair in his left hand. Roberto heard the click of a flick knife in his left ear, there was nothing he could do, his body felt lifeless. Rambo cut out a circular opening in the central area of the rattan seat. He violently stamped on Roberto's ribs then proceeded to strip his limp body. From his left jacket pocket he pulled a bag of black cable ties and began to secure Roberto's limbs to the chair.

Rambo stood in front of his battered, bruised and naked adversary. Blood poured from Roberto's nose and mouth. He'd been gagged using a thick piece of oil soaked rope. Out of his right jacket pocket Rambo produced a pair of chrome pliers. These were no conventional pliers though, the central mechanism had a medieval feel. Rambo gently squeezed the handles of the double-action, scissor-like instrument. The jaws opened, dilating a neon orange rubber ring. Roberto's eyeballs bulged with fear as he mumbled for his life. Rambo circled his hostage through 540 degrees. Roberto's heart beat quickened further. Other than the subtle sounds of stretching rubbing and squeaking metal, the room was eerily quiet. Rambo crouched in the darkness, composed as ever. He enjoyed seeing Roberto panic and suffer, it comforted him. In one fluid movement, he dropped to a knee. He tightly pinched Roberto's already contracted scrotum between his left thumb and index finger. He pulled firmly to create distance between Roberto's testicles and perineum. With a final squeeze, release and withdrawal, Roberto entered stage one of a protracted castration. He omitted a eunuch scream, his true suffering would only be heard by neighbouring dogs, such was its pitch.

The pain was unbearable; the rubber ring clamped, crushed, choked and burned. Rambo paced slowly, once again facing the abused Roberto. "I'm gonna give you and your fuckwit son one week to get out the city. If you don't, I'll end your family line for good. Smooth-talking businessman Frank isn't around anymore, I'm in charge, which means you're a nobody, a nothing." A trembling Roberto nodded silently. The agony of the experience causing his neck veins to protrude and swell.

The unflustered Rambo continued, "I'll drop your boy Robbie a text from your phone, asking him to come pick you up. Might be in an hour, might be in a day, depends how charitable I'm feeling. Enjoy packing your bags." A double slap on the cheek ended the ordeal, for Rambo anyway. He walked back to his pickup, selecting *Ring of Fire* as his next tune, adding insult to horrific injury. He lowered his window as he reversed out of the shed. A menacing smile was accompanied by a final statement, "goodbye Roberto." Rambo would wait until morning before texting Robbie. He needed this to be a proper statement of intent, an undeniable change of narrative.

CHAPTER 19

MISTAKEN IDENTITY

Thursday, 16th November 2023.

A disorientated James woke up in a private room. He'd been moved from the high dependency unit during the night. The chest wound should really have killed him, but for once, luck seemed to be on his side. The bullet had missed his aorta by 2mm but left powder burns on his heart. Officers Thom and Maguire were due to arrive at 9:30am, they'd waited three long weeks for his statement. James' bleary eyes scanned for a wall clock, which appeared to read 8:25am. A slight neck tilt brought on a thumping headache, which in part distracted him from the continuous pain pulsing through his body.

At the base of his bed, James could make out two seated figures. He winced as he attempted to prop himself up. From a slightly improved vantage point, a groggy James questioned, "You two are keen, no?"

"We just wanted to pop in and see how you were doing." James had been informed that both police officers would be male. The recognisable female voice completely threw him. James squinted and eventually found focus. "Amber?! What the hell you doing here?"

"I've just finished-" James cut her off mid sentence.

"Charlie! How you doing wee man?! It's so good to see you. Come give daddy a big hug." A further grimace as James grabbed his chest, too much, too soon it seemed. Amber replied, "Oh James, be careful. No, sorry, sorry James. This isn't Charlie, this is my little boy Lucas." James felt immediately conflicted, the boy was the double of Charlie in almost every way. After a few seconds of observation, Lucas was maybe an inch or two shorter, his beautiful curly hair was maybe a touch lighter, but it was hard for James to be sure.

Amber continued, "Charlie is completely safe, he's with your neighbour. He's been in to see you loads. He'll be buzzing to know that you are awake and able to talk. Little Lucas is only three, two years younger than your beautiful boy."

The situation, the information, it was all too much for the now discombobulated James to take in. He challenged his visitor, "Amber. Seriously. Gonna tell me why you're here?" Amber replied sharply, "Well, before you cut me off, I was going to say that I'd just finished a nightshift in accident and emergency. You've been the talk of this place the past few weeks! My mum dropped this one at the main door as we're about to go swimming. Got to keep busy you know, otherwise you pass out with fatigue! As I was leaving, one of the nurses told me that sleeping beauty had awakened! So yeah, thought I'd just nip up and say hi."

James was listening, of course he was, but he couldn't take his eyes off Lucas. "Well that's very kind of you Amber. Thank you so much."

"It's great seeing you again James, although I wish it could be under different circumstances." James gave an apologetic look. "Listen, sorry Amber. I should have contacted you after that night."

"Hey, don't you be silly Mr. That chat is for another day. You just focus on getting better! I'm sure our paths will cross again." James looked at Amber affectionately, yet again he felt a natural connection. "Really though Amber, it's so nice of you to come see me." James didn't want to ask the obvious question but he couldn't help himself, "So, eh, when's Lucas' birthday by the way?"

"Haha! I could hear the cogs turning James!" Don't panic big boy. We used protection, remember? And I don't have the gestation length of a donkey. Lucas was born July 2020, 14 months after CC Blooms!" James laughed, then coughed, then grimaced again. "Bloody chest."

Amber rose from her chair and buttoned up Lucas' winter coat. "Right James, we better head off, you'll be due your breakfast soon. Oh, just before I go though. Do you know who shot you?" A distinctive change of tone from Amber. James replied in a soft voice, "He was called Frank, I'm sure he gave his surname but I can't seem to remember it. I've tried and tried but-"

"Smith, his names Frank Smith," declared Amber. James' face flushed with colour, "How do you know that?"

"Oh James, every nurse and doctor in this place is talking about it, police officers are manning front reception 24/7. Frank Smith is one of the most notorious gangsters in Scotland. But, I never told you any of that, okay?"

"Yeah, yeah, course," replied James. "And sorry for questioning you about Lucas, he just looks a bit like my lad, that's all." Amber smiled, "No need to apologise, all kids look alike eh?! It'll soon be you who's batting away questions! Everyone's calling it mistaken identity, it seems you've just been really unlucky James. Wrong place, wrong time I guess."

Amber walked forward and kissed James on the forehead, "Rest up friend." She took Lucas by the hand and exited the room.

Breakfast arrived five minutes later. James managed to eat some porridge and drink some orange juice, a significant step forward in his recovery. Thom and Maguire arrived at 9:20am. As a trio, they discussed the night of Thursday 26th October. The conversation lasted almost two hours. James provided every piece of detail he possibly could, including a full description of the shooter and his first and last name. Both officers thanked him for his honesty and openness, they left feeling like prime Holmes and Watson.

As soon as his arse hit the passenger seat of their unmarked Astra, Maguire spouted, "Ya fucking dancer! We've got him!" Thom smiled, then replied, "It's looking good, but remember what the boss said. Airtight."

The discussion had emptied the already frail James, so many scarring emotions and memories. He slept until dinner time. Over the course of several days, James slowly regained some strength and confidence. Physiotherapists and nurses took him through various rehabilitation programmes. He was eventually deemed fit to return home and was discharged on Monday, 27th November 2023. He'd been in hospital for 31 days.

CHAPTER 20

ROGUES' GALLERY

Friday, 3rd November 2023.

Lucas gave Steph a big hug, "Goodbye Auntie Steph, love you." Steph smiled proudly, "I love you more magic man, you be sure to look after mummy for me, yeah?" The youngster responded with a beaming smile. Amber thanked Steph for her kindness and hospitality, she kissed her on the cheek before unlocking her car. The long drive home would give her an opportunity to reflect on the past few days. What Frank did to James was no doubt extreme, but, it simply joined a long line of historical atrocities. Frank's actions stopped shocking her a long time ago, their journey from heaven to hell had numbed her. As she approached Dundee, Amber scanned over her shoulder. Paw Patrol continued to play on the iPad, but Lucas had long drifted off to sleep. She carefully reached behind and muted the device. The straight road and almost perfect silence settled her into her own prolonged daydream.

Amber found herself replaying several interactions in her head. Each one reminded her of Frank's ability to influence and intimidate. His words were etched in her memory. Amber's mind focused on the very first time they met. A wet day in August 2015. Frank casually wandered into her gallery. She recalled her first impressions of him: he was striking: handsome and mysterious in equal measure. He spent several minutes perusing through her work. She wanted to ask if he needed assistance but felt unusually nervous. Amber assumed he would simply look then leave as most do. But no. Frank eventually approached the counter, "Good morning," Smiled Amber.

"Morning. I'd like two things please."

"Oh yeah? And what are they?"

"Well first of all, I'd like to take you out for dinner."

"Haha! Wow! You eh, you don't mess around do you?" Spouted Amber. Frank smiled, "If I see something I like, I just have to have it." His supreme confidence immediately intrigued her. "And what was the second thing?"

"I'd like to buy some paintings off you."

"Well that I can do that, no problem at all. And... your name is?"

"Sorry, how rude of me! Frank, My name is Frank."

"Well Frank, Which ones are you interested in?"

"All of them!"

Amber laughed awkwardly, she was flattered, but confused. Frank continued. "I'll take that one to get the ball rolling, bring it over." He pointed at a framed original on the back wall. "Eh, yeah, okay, sure. Ticket price on that is £750." Frank produced a roll of notes from his coat pocket. He counted out £800 and said, "keep the change partner." Amber replied hesitantly, "goodness, cash? Thank you very much."

"I'll pick you up at 7:00pm."

"What? Tonight!? So you're being serious?" Laughed Amber.

"You don't even know where I live you madman."

"Yeah I do. See you at seven."

Amber's confusion and curiosity only grew. "Wear a nice dress." A confident wink accompanied Frank's instruction. "Okay, yeah, sure." Amber nodded her head in agreement. As she started to prep the painting, Frank simply walked away. "Hey, where are you going?"

"I've got a meeting in 20 minutes. You bubble wrap the painting and bring it tonight. See you later." Frank was gone before Amber could respond again.

Conversation flowed over pre-dinner drinks. Each glass of wine brought increased sexual chemistry. Amber hadn't felt such a buzz in years. Her and Frank just seemed to connect on so many levels. But, as soon as the meal began, Frank returned to pure business mode. "I have a proposal for you." A tipsy Amber giggled, "Oh Frank, we've only just met!"

"Let's get real for a minute Amber eh? What if I told you we could make life changing money?" Amber popped her glass on the table and smiled, "I did wonder what you meant by partner earlier! I'm listening Frank."

"You're an artist Amber, and a very good one at that. But, you and I both know, it's fucking murder trying to make big profits. What if I was to join you as a silent partner in your business?" Amber laughed, "Me and you?"

"No no, hear me out. With me on board your sales figures would immediately rocket, and your work would gain huge exposure."

"Sorry Frank, I'm not following you here, maybe it's the wine, maybe it's my lack of business accruement, indulge me."

"Okay. Take today for example, I bought a piece of art from you, legitimately for £800. What if that piece of art was suddenly worth £5000? You'd bank the 5k, the taxman takes his share, we than cut what's left in an agreed split. A significant proportion of your initial sales would be through our arrangement, but with quality marketing and social media advertising, I reckon the business could have a legitimate feel within three years."

"Okay, let's slow down and rewind a touch shall we?" Amber leaned towards Frank, scanning the room for pricked ears. She whispered to him, "So let me get this right. You're a fucking gangster? Who's trying to launder money through my little art gallery? She sighed disappointingly, "Fuck me."

Frank bit back quietly, "Let's not play the affronted card Amber eh. I'm giving you an opportunity to make serious money here, a chance to change your life forever. Daddy's allowance has dried up, mummy's done all she can. How many paintings you sold in your first six months?"

Amber's tone immediately changed. She snarled, "Don't you ever talk about my fucking parents, alright? And don't pretend you know me. I don't like that." Frank replied, "Well, I'm glad I've got your attention now. Let me give you a chance to love this. Answer my question, how many paintings?" A fuming Amber responded, "Today was my eighteenth sale since opening." Frank sniggered, "18?! Jesus Christ, three units a months. The highest ticket item I saw today was £750. Best case scenario, you're making 27k a year on that sales pattern. For someone so talented that's fucking horrible Amber. Making rent will quickly become your biggest priority and obstacle. Work with me and you could be making 27k a month, then 27k a fucking week. That's footballer wages. All we need to do initially is create a sales narrative, then promote and scale-" Amber interjected, "So, essentially you're going to buy my art using your cash? Except it isn't my art anymore, is it? It's our art as we'd be fucking partners? You then claim back your own money once it's been washed and taxed? And you own a painting that you don't really want or need, and in truth, it was fucking yours to begin with!"

"Pretty much darling! But, with a bonus caveat. I'll be hanging any pieces I love in my house, and there are plenty, thereafter, most will stay in the gallery to be sold again and again. That way, you aren't working like a handmaid producing painting after painting. As I say, if we get the marketing right, daft rich cunts will take note of your name and numbers, legitimate sales will increase simultaneously. Legitimate sales go through as card transitions, providing some traceability, but the majority of your business will be cash deals. That's commonplace in the art world and won't be seriously challenged. It can't fail Amber. What do you think?"

"I think I need another bottle of wine." Replied Amber.

Amber knew she couldn't let her business fail, Gayle's investment was indeed about to end. She had to prove to her prick father that she could be a success in her own right, choosing her own career. She thought to herself, *how bad an idea could this be?* After more discussion and much more alcohol, Frank produced an official partnership agreement. Max had mocked it up that afternoon. They both signed on the dotted line. From that moment, Amber belonged to Frank.

Lucas woke up from his nap as they reached the Forth Road Bridge. Nursery songs played them home. As Amber pulled into her drive she was met by a team of uniformed officers. Skinner and McMullan were immediately radioed.

CHAPTER 21

THE TROPHY WIFE

Sunday, 26th May 2019.

The power Frank wielded that night at the dinner table was a clear indication of things to come. But, nothing could prepare Amber for the evil that followed. In the early months of their partnership, Amber enjoyed being a key driver in Frank's powerful organisation. As time progressed, their business relationship also became sexual. Everything was kept low key for a number of personal and security reasons. Very few people knew they were an item, and even less knew they lived together. Private matters remained private, that was until Frank made clear that he wanted a family in early 2018. Amber was less than sure.

As time wore on Frank's psyche at home became more unstable, his behaviour more erratic. He dragged Amber from specialist to specialist in a bid to improve their fertility. His constant want for a family turned into his constant need for a family. The more desperate he became, the more repulsed Amber felt. But she couldn't get out, she couldn't escape. Such was his dominance.

Frank had arranged for a cosy night in. He ordered Chinese from their favourite takeaway, it was to arrive at 6:15pm. He was already irritated, the time had just passed 6:00pm and Amber still wasn't home from the gym. He set the table and poured two large glasses of Pinot Grigio. That second, Amber bounded in the front door. "What fucking time do you call this?" Spouted Frank.

"Sorry babe, traffic was wild. I'm here now though!" Frank scowled, "I suppose so, go grab a quick shower then."

"No way! I'm starving, I'll grab a shower after." Replied Amber. Frank muttered under his breath, "Fuck sake."

"What did you say?" Challenged Amber.
Before he could reply, the doorbell rang. "I'll get it," said Frank. He returned almost immediately with a confused look on his face. He placed the food onto the kitchen table and glared at Amber. "Is that a new mirror at the front door?" Amber took a seat, attempting to ignore the question. "Did you hear me Amber?"

"Sorry darling, what's that?" There was an obvious nervous tone to her voice.

"I said, that's a new mirror at the front door." No longer a question, now a statement. Amber laughed awkwardly, "What you talking about honey?"

"Honey?! Don't fuckin honey me! The other one had a chip in the frame, I kept meaning to fill it."

"Gees, I'm not sure Frank." Frank snapped, "Don't lie to me!" He let out a scream, then lifted and tipped the kitchen table onto its side. Kung Po, Chow mein and prawn crackers flew across the kitchen, the individual containers exploding on impact. Frank grabbed Amber by her ponytail, jerking her head backwards violently as she sat on her chair. His mouth a centimetre from her left ear; he whispered sinisterly, "Listen cunt, I made you, and I can just as easily break you. What have I told you about fucking lying?"

"Frank, please, you're hurting me." Responded a quivering Amber, her voice filled with trepidation. Frank pulled Amber closer still, his right hand gripping her hair like a vice, his wandering left hand forcefully slipping into her sports bra, fondling her breasts. "Please, no, don't do this."

"Don't do what Amber, don't do what? You're gonna slip your leggings off and bend over that sofa, like a good little girl, and you're gonna fuckin love it, aren't you?"

"Frank, baby, I've just been working out, please-" Before she could even finish her begging sentence, Frank exploded, "Hurry the fuck up! Legs spread on the living room sofa, you're my little slut." A sobbing Amber obliged, what choice did she have? A now rabid Frank was incensed by her geriatric pace, he stepped forward and painfully yanked at her thong, ripping it from her body. He then forced her half lowered leggings to her ankles before throwing her onto the sofa. He spat on himself and forcefully entered Amber. She winced in pain. "How we gonna get pregnant if you don't want to fuck eh? Stupid cunt." Amber was submissive and emotionless throughout. Frank finished inside, he always did. He pulled up his trousers and walked back through to the kitchen, slamming the door so hard that it shut and reopened. He sat on one of the four kitchen chairs. Staring coldly at the distant mirror. Amber could be heard sobbing in the next room, a haunting sound.

After a few seconds, Frank got up and walked back through to where she lay. But, no apology came, only more abuse. "Since I can't trust a fucking word you say, I'll be monitoring exactly what and who comes through my fucking front door from now on. There'll be a camera installed by breakfast time tomorrow. And another thing, how do you think you make a baby you daft cunt? You used to be a proper girl, nothing was off limits. Now it's fucking nightdress missionary pish. Am fucking bored wi you. Am away out, get that fucking mess cleaned up. Amber didn't move, she didn't speak, she just wanted him to leave."

Amber limped upstairs and into the shower. The pain was severe, yet, the overriding feeling was disbelief. After drying herself, she put on clean pyjamas and slippers, then packed an overnight bag. She refused to clean up, and she certainly wasn't willing to wait around for him to return. She hurriedly locked up, got in her Mini and drove straight back to Aberdeen. Steph left the front door open. Amber walked straight in and collapsed on Steph's bed. She wept, "I can't keep living like this Steph." Steph nodded and hugged her tight. Amber could hold her own with most, but not this version of Frank. His heart was dark, his soul empty. In sociopath mode, he truly was a monster: egotistical, immoral and uncontrollably violent. Steph sat Amber up and looked her straight in the eye, "It's time for your revenge Amber. We've started the process, all you need to do is keep yourself safe. I'll take care of everything else. We already know he's too powerful to leave, too smart to frame, too well connected to kill. This is how it must be done."

CHAPTER 22

BREAKFAST NEWS

Friday, 20th October 2023.

Amber and Steph met for drinks on George Street. A catch up was long overdue. They hadn't seen each other in 16 months, Lucas' second birthday party to be exact. The detachment was very deliberate, Steph wanted nothing to do with Frank. She also felt it was safer for Amber if she distanced herself from the relationship.

Despite the significant time apart, conversation flowed naturally, it always did. They joked and laughed their way through several cocktails and a bottle of red wine. But, eventually Steph had to ask the question, "So, how are things now? Please be honest with me." Amber smiled, "Truthfully Steph, much better. Yeah he's still unpredictable, he has bad days, but, Lucas has changed him, like genuinely changed him. They play together day and night. Almost every weekend they're at soft play or swimming, nothing gets in the way." Steph responded, "So Frank's a nominee for father of the year is he? That's great to hear, but what about you?" A more sombre reply from Amber, "It's still dysfunctional, but, becoming a mother means I'm no longer expendable, which is reassuring. Frank knows my worth beyond business now. We've agreed that we have a shared responsibility to give Lucas an amazing life. Steph nodded her head, "Proud of you. But, please, promise me, if you ever find yourself in danger again, you come to me, yeah?" Amber winked, "Of course, you're my number one, cheers."

The pair chugged back the last few gulps of their wine. That very moment, Amber's phone buzzed. A text from Frank. "Heading to bed. Lucas has been down for two hours. Have a great night. Love you x." Amber showed Steph the message, "Wow, look, some affection!" Steph laughed sarcastically, "Let's not read too deep into a text eh!" Amber immediately changed the tone of the conservation, "Hey, he said have a great night! It's only 10:30pm. Let's bounce to another bar and see where we end up eh?" Yet again, Steph reeled her back in. "Sounds great. But just so we're clear, Frank's definitely away in the morning yeah? I'm not making small talk around the kitchen table Amber. Don't get me wrong, I'm happy things are amicable now, but, I'll never forgive him for what he did to you. I'm sorry, but he still makes my skin crawl." Amber replied, "Yes babe, he's on a 5:50am flight tomorrow morning, you won't even see him, trust me."

Frank brushed his teeth then gargled mouthwash. He got into bed and turned off his bedside lamp. A few minutes later his phone rang, he answered silent. "Boss, you there?" Frank sighed, "Fuck sake Rambo, what is it?" Rambo replied hesitantly, "Listen, I know you've got the wee man, but this is kinda urgent, there's a major problem with a shipment." Frank moaned, "Surely to fuck it can wait till the morning."

"Aren't you away to Holland boss?" A further irritated sigh from Frank, "Christ, yeah, yeah I am. Right, well, I canni bring Lucas with me. How long's this gonna take?"

"Couple of hours I'd guess."

Frank threw on the first suit he could find. He checked on Lucas then left the house in a hurry. As he drove he wondered if he should call Amber. If she got home before him she'd be livid, and rightly so. His brain started to play tricks on him. *What if Lucas wakes up alone and is terrified? What if he falls down the stairs? What if he somehow unlocks the front door and wanders out to the street?* He chastised himself, "Fuck off Frank, switch on, get this fixed then straight back home." He reckoned Amber and Steph would be out all night, both loved to socialise and hadn't seen each other for so long.

Amber and Steph staggered through the front door just after 1:00am. They giggled and snorted as they attempted to kick off their shoes. Amber hung both their coats over a kitchen chair. "Shh-shh-shh, Steph, be quiet! Frank and Lucas are sound asleep remember, go through to the living room. I'll fix us a nightcap, gin and tonic all good?" An already blotto Steph responded with a merry smile and a double thumbs up. She really didn't need anything else.

Amber turned on the living room floor lamp, then dimmed its brightness using an app on her phone. The pair slumped onto the sofa, but only seconds later, Steph was back on her unsteady feet. She spouted, "Oh my god!" Then stumbled across the room and picked up a family photograph. A frustrated Amber whispered through gritted teeth. "Steph! What did I say? Be quiet." Steph produced a mumbled reply, "Amber, how grown up does Lucas look? He's the absolute double of James! Fucking hell, that's mental. I've never noticed it before. He's changed so much over the last wee while. Can't wait to see him in the morning." Amber interjected, grabbing Steph by the shoulders. "Steph, shut the fuck up! You've already said too much."

"Whoopsie! Sorry babe. No more, I promise." But, the damage had already been done. Frank stood in the shadows of the upstairs landing, he'd overheard every spoken word. He'd only got home five minutes before the drunken duo. He was faced with two options, address the matter head on or sneak back to bed. He decided the latter made more sense. He turned slowly and tiptoed towards his bedroom.

Amber woke up at 9:30am. She immediately craved a glass of water and two paracetamol. She stared at herself in the ensuite mirror, *a cocktail too many*, she thought. For once, Lucas hadn't been in to wake her. An attempted lie in was often met with kangaroo bounces and swan dives to the solar plexus! She wasn't concerned though, she could hear him singing and laughing downstairs as his favourite songs played through the Sonos system. She assumed Steph was making the most of her morning with him. Whilst slipping on some loungewear, Amber shouted, "Steph, I'll just be two minutes babe."

She casually walked downstairs and into the kitchen, but was stopped in her tracks. She shrieked, "Frank! What you doing here?"

"I live here, don't I?" A condescending response.

Amber replied nervously, "Sorry darling. It's just, I thought you had an early flight? A meeting in Amsterdam, no?" He responded abruptly, "Flight was cancelled."

"Oh, really? Well, that's annoying."

Amber scanned the room, "Where's eh, where's Steph?" She peered at the kitchen chair, Steph's coat was gone. "She said she had to get back to Aberdeen, she had lots to do apparently." Amber frowned faintly in confusion, "Yeah, she's a busy girl alright."

Frank instructed Lucas to run through to his playroom, he'd set up some of his favourite toys as a distraction. Amber's lack of eye contact and finger fidgeting had already confirmed to Frank that Steph's drunken comments carried considerable weight. As soon as the youngster left the room, Frank turned up the volume on his phone, The Wiggles boomed through the downstairs stereos. Frank picked up a mug of coffee from the kitchen worktop and took a big step forward, his sudden movement startled Amber.

"Why you so nervous? I've made you a nice coffee, great for a hangover. Why don't you take a seat."
Amber did as instructed, producing a forced smile, "Oh, thanks darling." But, before the mug reached the table, a loaded question. "Who's James?" Amber knew she'd be forced to make eye contact. Frank gazed at her through narrowed, darkened eyes. It was a look of pure hatred. "Frank, please-"
She was cut off immediately.
"I said, who's James?"

"Frank, I can't-" With a flick of Frank's right wrist, coffee splashed onto Amber's chest, her skin was scalded. She screamed out in pain and shock, jumping to her feet. But, as she tried to remove her burning top, an enraged Frank attacked. He grabbed her by the throat and drove her backwards against the patio door. Amber gasped for breath, the more she struggled the tighter his grip became. Frank continued to squeeze, pushing the back of her head and neck against the glass, she could feel her trachea tearing under the pressure. Fighting back was useless, she tried to reason with him but her words were replaced by a desperate whimper. Just as she was losing consciousness, Frank released his grip. She fell to the floor, choking and coughing, whilst desperately trying to take in air.

After several seconds, Amber sat up against the glass door. Tears streamed down her face. Her first thought was Lucas, *please don't walk in, you don't deserve to see this*. Frank stood over her, his fists clenched. "Now's your chance Amber. Be careful with your next words, they could be your last." Amber was utterly defenceless. She knew she was in a kill or be killed situation, she had no choice. "It's not what you think Frank, on my life, it's not what you think. I promise you, just hear me out."

"I just need to know one thing Amber, am I Lucas' dad?"
Amber dropped her head and stared at the floor, "I hope so Frank, I really do." Frank fell to his knees, feelings of rage were replaced

by disbelief. He placed both his hands on Amber's shoulders and shook her, "What do you mean you hope so?" Amber sobbed.

"I was raped Frank, James Riley raped me. He came to one of my art exhibitions, I knew his face from university, but couldn't place him. He seemed genuinely interested in my work. We'd all had a few wines so I decided to walk home rather than risk driving. He waited for me to lock up, followed me, then attacked." Frank shook his head and snarled, "No. No. No. You're a liar, that's a fucking lie." Amber responded bluntly, "I wish it was Frank." After seconds of silent thought. Frank continued, his voice breaking with emotion, "So, you're telling me that Lucas isn't my boy? And this cunt James raped you on the street?" A defiant Amber bit back, she took strength from Frank's vulnerability. "No Frank, listen to what I am saying, he might not be yours. At the time, you and I both wanted to conceive so badly. For whatever reason, we couldn't. I guess the dream of having a little one superseded the shame of what James did. I wanted to tell you but I couldn't find the courage. I've always believed that Lucas was your boy, our boy." Frank stared Amber in the eyes, "He's a fucking dead man."

An angry Amber replied, "Don't you fucking dare say that. After everything you've done. You can't judge anyone. I know it's a horrible thought, but nothing changes, Lucas is ours. I told Steph to shut up last night, not to keep a secret from you, but because I can't keep revisiting that fucking night. James is the devil, not me, not you. We have to move forward for the greater good of the family."

Frank paused, then shook his head again. "Fuck off Amber, I can't accept that, you know I can't. I've got to know, this will hang over me forever otherwise. We need a paternity test, now. You get a shower, I'll call around some clinics. If I'm the dad after all this, okay, we can talk about it and maybe move on. If this James is the dad, there's a bullet with his name on it."

Frank stood up, grabbed his phone and immediately started searching for private clinics. Amber remained seated, Frank's final comments sent her into a panicked daze. She tried to process the consequences of the conversation she had just facilitated. A burnt chest and damaged throat were the least of her worries.

Thursday, 26th October 2023.

Frank had waited five long days for the results. He'd barely spoke to Amber in that time, the tension between the two was unbearable. His phone buzzed at 9:05am. He opened the email, then scrolled and scanned. The final sentence made him feel physically sick. A life changing statement, "Probability of paternity 0%." Frank silently passed the phone to Amber for confirmation. She begged, "Frank please, let's consider all our options here, don't jump into something we could all regret." Frank ignored her, it was like she'd been placed on mute. Instead he picked the phone out of her hand and immediately called Max. "You got that address for me Max? Send it through now." Frank looked at Amber, "Consequences must match the actions Amber. Now kindly run along and rehearse our agreed alibi. This cunt dies tonight."

A horrific realisation entered Amber's mind. She'd orchestrated the killing of the only man she'd ever loved. It was madness. Why should James die just so she could live? She frantically processed how she could somehow intervene without exposing herself.

CHAPTER 23

ANIMAL INSTINCTS

Saturday, 2nd December 2023.

James' fifth day recuperating at home having been discharged from hospital. The ever dependable Carol waited on him hand and foot. Reluctantly, Martin okayed Carol's relocation to number 39 to support James' rehabilitation, but, only for a week. Charlie had been without his daddy for a full month, and Martin knew that Carol's presence would aid paternal transition and connection. His constantly ruminating brain figured the maimed James wouldn't have a ride in him for some time, so Carol and his marriage should be safe. Plus, the pair would rarely be alone due to the volume of visiting care workers and physiotherapists. Oh, and Martin would be sure to drop in every day after work just to make sure services remained medicinal. James still had a four week course of painkillers to get through; walking, lying and sleeping remained painful activities.

In truth, Martin's troubles and worries were all created in his own head. Whilst he worshipped Carol, he had always had a feeling that she could be more, do more, and that perhaps she had settled for mediocrity. Nothing could be further from the truth though. Not once had Carol even considered cheating on him, and certainly not with James. Yes, she loved him unconditionally, no doubt, but it was purely platonic. Feelings from James had been mutual throughout their long friendship.

As always, Carol wanted to normalise Charlie's experience. She'd arranged to take Sarah and Charlie to Edinburgh Zoo for the afternoon. This would allow James further rest time. He'd planned to watch Burnley versus Sheffield United in the English Premier

League. Rachel was originally from Burnley, James and her had attended a few games at Turf Moor when visiting her family. Over the years, Burnley had become his second team, and since he'd just been given a second shot at life, he figured he should start doing things he enjoyed with more regularity.

Carol and a very excited Charlie set off for the zoo at 2pm, they would return around 6pm. James settled onto the sofa and looked forward to an afternoon of relaxation and entertainment. As the referee blew for half-time, James joked to himself that his luck might be turning! Burnley were 2-0 up and McBurnie had been sent off for Sheffield.

He gingerly reached over and picked up his phone from the ash grey coffee table. "How's my boy doing?" Messaged James. Two minutes later, a photo response from Carol. The beautiful Charlie grinning from ear to ear, a 200 kilogram silverback in the background. "Having the best time daddy, hope you're chilling?" A contented James smiled. "I am that. Have the best time, thanks again Carol. J x." James sat his phone on the right arm of the sofa and took a sip of water.

The second half was attack versus defence, the lack of competition slipped James into a peaceful nap. He awoke with six minutes left to play. He'd missed three goals, Burnley now led 5-0. He picked up his phone again, using Face ID to unlock the keypad. Carol had sent a further nine photos, showcasing the trios adventurous afternoon out. James proudly scrolled through each of them. Until he flicked onto photo number eight.

An exhausted Carol secured Charlie into his car seat. She'd forgotten how steep a hike Edinburgh Zoo was, particularly with a zestful and equally indecisive five-year-old. Sarah popped their rucksacks into the boot. Both fastened their seatbelts and breathed a sigh of relief, it had been a brilliantly chaotic three hours. What fun they'd had, Carol was proud of Sarah, she'd played and interacted with Charlie nonstop. Now it was time for dinner and down time. As her dashboard clock ticked past 5:30pm, Carol scanned to her right, the exit queue was huge. She glanced in her mirror, Charlie had fallen asleep almost instantly, he gripped Mr Sheepy tightly in his right hand, head tilted, eyes rolling back, mouth wide open. "I'll text James just so he knows we are on route," said Carol.

"No worries," replied Sarah.

"Oh wow!"

"What's up?"

"I've six missed calls from James, hope he's okay. I better call instead." A jittery James answered within two rings. "Who you at the zoo with?" A startling question.

"What do you mean James?" Replied a confused Carol.

"The wee boy, beside Charlie at the tiger den, who is he?"

"Who? Lucas? Just one of his wee pals. How come?"

"How can Charlie and Lucas be pals Carol? Charlie is five, Lucas is only three."

"They've known each other for a while James, they've played a lot together over the last year or so." Carol paused. "Wait, how do you know Lucas?" James ignored the question. Responding instead with, "What do you mean they've played a lot? When? Where?"

"James, please, tell me, what's happening-?"

James interjected, "What's his mum's name?"

"James, what-"

James snapped, "What's her fucking name Carol?!"

"Amber! Why? James this is so out of character, are you okay?" Her question was met with heavy, panicked breathing. "We just bumped into them randomly James, it's been a great wee afternoon. Please, calm down. Please. Amber and I have been running pals for years, she's lovely."

"What? What the fuck you talking about Carol?" Asked James. Before she could respond, James jumped in with another set of questions. "Does Amber know who Charlie is Carol? Does she know me?"

"James, what's with the crazy interrogation?" A now manic James bit again, "Just answer my fucking questions Carol!"

"Okay okay, no need to shout and swear, you're on loudspeaker in the car. I was only blooming calling to say we're on our way back and to check how you were feeling. Obviously she knows Charlie, yes. But, no, she doesn't know you. Funny though, she's always joking about how handsome you are. She often asks to see pictures of you and Charlie. Anyway, Charlie is sleeping, we will be home in about half an hour. Talk more then, okay? Please chill out and calm down." James eventually softened his tone, "Okay, okay, sorry. See you then. But, Carol, we need to discuss this further, tonight."

"Agreed," responded Carol. "See you soon."

James hung up the phone and whispered to himself, "Doesn't know me eh?" So many emotions flooded his body; confusion, anger, fear, anxiety to list a few.

Carol parked outside number 39. "Sarah, honey, before we go in, please be aware that James is under a lot of pressure right now with his recovery and upcoming court case. You know how lovely he is, he's on strong medication and it's taking its toll." Sarah nodded her head, she was still processing the bizarre phone call. Carol opened the front door at 6:07pm. She didn't ring the doorbell, she no longer needed to, James had given her a key whilst he was hospitalised. She was followed closely by Sarah, carrying an exhausted Charlie.

The first thing that caught Carol's attention was the aroma of baked lasagne and garlic bread. Chill-out music played in the kitchen, James had set the table for four people. She felt relieved, James had obviously felt well enough, and indeed calm enough to make dinner for everyone. But his next instruction heightened her

worry again. "Sarah, would you mind running a bath for Charlie pal? Your mum and I need to have a chat, alone."
"Yeah, course, see you guys soon," replied Sarah.

Carol had hoped the important conversation would be a post dinner event. But, it was clear from James' fidgeting that he was agitated and apprehensive, he wanted to proceed immediately. As Sarah and Charlie reached the upstairs landing, James invited Carol to join him at the kitchen table. "Right, Carol. I need to piece together what the fuck is going on here."
"Going on? I wish I knew James," replied Carol.

"Yes, yes. I get it, you've been blindsided too, but I will try to explain. First things first. You got any pictures of Amber?"

"Yeah tonnes, I'll show you," said Carol.

Carol got out her phone and passed it to James. He chuckled nervously as he flicked through her camera roll. "I'm sorry James, you'll need to help me out here. Who's blindsided me? I have no idea what you're talking about, remember. Amber and I are friends." James launched a new barrage of questions.
"How long have you known each other Carol?"

"Gees, I don't know, six, maybe seven years."

"Jesus fucking Christ," James took a deep breath to compose himself. "Does she have a husband?"

"A partner yes, he's a successful businessman, he's also called James, believe it or not, but everyone calls him Jim. She doesn't mention him much though, he's often out the country on business."

"You're right, I don't fucking believe it. Ever seen a picture of him?"

"Now you mention it, no, she's never shown me."

"And where does she live?"

"My word James Riley, I think I'll need to rename you Hercule Poirot!" An irritated James bit once more, "Carol! Come on, help me out here."

"Sorry, apologies. She lives in the New Town. That I know to be true, she's sent me pictures of her house, it's incredible, a gorgeous home. I assumed she's from money."

"Show me please," asked James. "Fuck me man."

He continued, "Listen, Carol. I trust you, always have done. What I'm about to tell you is gonna sound fucking mental." James clasped his hands on top of his placemat, in a desperate bid to stop involuntary squirming. "You know what? I need a beer, fancy a bottle?"

"Eh, yeah, sure." Replied a hesitant Carol. "You stay put, I'll get them. You've already done far too much today. And, you're only having one mind, those are strong painkillers you're on." James took a sip of his Peroni. "So, Amber. She has no idea who I am eh?"

"So she says," replied Carol. "The last couple of years we've joked that you two would make a gorgeous couple, but, she's obviously got a man. And, to be clear, we were always joking James, I'd never disrespect Rachel like that." James smiled and shook his head despondently. "Carol. Amber and I first met in two thousand and fucking eleven. That's right, 12 years ago, long before Rachel was on the scene."

"What?!" Inquired a shocked Carol. "Why in gods name wouldn't she have said?"

"Because Carol, she's been playing you. Something fucked up is happening here. Remember that lads day Martin organised back in 2019? Hibs versus Aberdeen?"

"Yeah, vaguely, what about it?"

"Well, I randomly bumped into her again that night up the town." Carol's mind was full of confused thoughts. "James see when you say, first met and bumped into. What we talking?" James snapped back. "Sex Carol. We had this mad connection, the second time even stronger than the first. The night of the Hibs game, Rachel had only been dead seven months. I knew it was wrong, I wanted to go home, I really did, but I couldn't distance myself from her. She was like a fucking temptress."

“Where exactly did you meet James? What happened?”

“Just at the main bar in CC Blooms. She took me back to her bit in the New Town, the same minted place you just showed me. She’s a doctor as you know. But, even so, what a house.” Carol laughed. “Who’s a doctor? Amber? Amber’s an art dealer.” A further grimace smile from James and another swig of beer. “You’re sure Carol?”

“100%, I’ve been to her gallery! It’s on Frederick Street. I have three of her paintings on my living room wall.”

“Carol, she fucking visited me in hospital. Claiming to have just finished a nightshift in another ward. That’s how I recognised Lucas straight away from your WhatsApp photos, she bloody brought him with her.”

“Wow, James this is mental, you need to speak with her immediately, I’m just the middle man here. I’ll send you her number right now. Should you not be calling the police too?”

“Don’t bother sending it, I’ve already got it. Had it for four years but never used it, not once.” A perplexed Carol replied with a simple, “Okay.”

“And please Carol, cut ties with her. Not a fucking word of this conversation gets back to her. I need to find out what the fuck this thing is up to.”

Carol’s heart sank, she wanted to tell James just how well established her friendship with Amber was, but she couldn’t bring herself to do it, she simply replied, “Yeah, of course. Gees I’m not sure I’m hungry now James.” James replied, “Na, me neither, I feel sick. I’ll call the kids down, I’m sure they’re starving.”

James stood tall at snail’s pace, he shouted upstairs, “Sarah, Charlie, dinner is ready.” Charlie responded, “coming daddy.”

As he dished up dinner, James could only think of one thing, his impending phone call with Amber.

CHAPTER 24

WALKIE TALKIES

Sunday, 3rd December 2023.

After a restless night of overthinking, Carol made breakfast for everyone. For the first time in their long friendship there was an awkwardness between James and Carol. Both shattered adults used Charlie to facilitate innocent conversation. After finishing his toast and yogurt, Charlie left the table to go play in his toy room. During a period of silence, Carol thought to herself, Martin better not drop in right now, he's definitely gonna think we've screwed this time. James eventually broke the silence, "Listen Carol, I think we both need some breathing space on this. Thank you so much for everything you've done, you've been amazing, but I need time to process this whole situation."

The Amber bombshell had clearly disturbed both of them, but, for the already fretful James, his anxiety had reached new heights. He didn't want to doubt Carol, he really didn't, but cynicism was a natural response to this latest twist. Carol felt conflicted, she had been betrayed by Amber, she felt deeply sorry for James, yet was disappointed by his reaction to her. After clearing away mugs, plates and cutlery, she hugged and kissed Charlie then returned home, two days earlier than initially planned.

Seconds after walking through her front door, Carol was met by a bounding Jeff. His reaction immediately changed her mood. She crouched down to pet him, his thrashing tail swung his hips like a sidewinder rattlesnake. He wanted clapped so badly but his sheer excitement made it impossible to stand in one set position. For Jeff, six days without his mum had felt like six months, her return was pure ecstasy. After a minute of pure canine affection, Carol called upstairs for Martin and Sarah. Then she remembered, Hibs were playing Aberdeen at Easter Road, how ironic.

She entered the kitchen and made herself a coffee, Jeff followed every footstep, eventually joining her on the living room sofa. He snuggled in tightly and inhaled a deep breath of contentment. Carol sipped her black coffee and pondered whether several years of friendship had been a lie. Had she merely been a pawn in Amber's fucked up game? She tried to recall the exact date they first met. "Bingo!" Carol jumped to her feet, startling Jeff. She ran to the downstairs cupboard to find her diaries. They lived on a dusty shelf, ordered chronologically for easy access. Her entries took her right back to the very moment and location, she instantly felt sick. Amber was one conniving bitch.

Sunday 9th July, 2017.

The summer sun bloomed on the horizon; transforming cold, dark nooks into bright, inviting heat traps. The morning dew that had soaked Carol's feet and Jeff's paws on route, slowly evaporated as the sunlight crept over paths, trees and grassy areas. The time was 5:47am. Carol stood proudly on the summit of Arthur's Seat. She could see for miles, an unspoilt 360degree view of the iconic Edinburgh skyline. With a sharp intake of breath, she filled her lungs with fresh, cool Scottish air. It made her feel so alive, and so appreciative of her current circumstances.

Carol had brought a note pad and pencil with her. She'd hoped the glorious weather, picturesque view and silent privacy would inspire her writing. James and Rachel's wedding was only 48 days away; Saturday, 26th August. She wanted her speech to be perfect, to capture the love and admiration both felt for each other. She threw down a travel rug and poured a hot black coffee from her flask, hoping to continue from where she'd left off the week before. Jeff chewed down on a jumbo meat bone. He was only 11 months old but was already biddable and trustworthy. Carol was very comfortable with him having a solo wander as she wrote and rehearsed. Arthur's Seat was the greatest place Jeff had ever seen; full of flying wildlife, sticks, rocks and endless puddles. Both were so content, it was their own private playground at that time of day.

Jeff spent the next five minutes marking his territory; protecting his pack like an apex wolf, there was barely a bush he hadn't pissed on. Once he was confident that his mum was safe from any predators; he took a leisurely stroll down the south side path, referred to as the 'red route' by local walkers. It was deemed to be the steepest and most challenging of the half-dozen accent options, not that the sure footed Jeff cared. The red route offered amazing views over to the Salisbury Crags; a smaller, but equally as stunning vantage point from which to admire the city. Jeff spotted a flickering, colourful butterfly further down the path and decided that he was the man to catch it. He jumped, and bounced, and ran, and barked but this thing was illusive!

Jeff's moment of naive distraction had left him wide open to an ambush or surprise attack. Chomp! From nowhere, a fellow canine pounced on him, the initial impact startled and panicked Jeff. *Was this real?* Luckily for him, the assailant was a fine natured labradoodle, called Brian. Brian's mouth was soft and gentle, he growled jovially, playfully goading Jeff to fight back. Both dogs reared onto their hind legs; they resembled punch-drunk boxers, vying for ring position in the final round of a world title bout. Then, out of nowhere, both powered into a sprint start. Their muscular legs propelling them towards the summit, it was a mad dash to the finish, as if one of them had whispered to the other "Ready, set, go."

The racing dogs gave Carol such a fright. "Oh my god Jeff, what are you up to? And who's your daft pal? Aren't you gorgeous buddy." Jeff and Brian circulated Carol; tails wagging, tongues hanging, both pleading for attention. Jeff was sure he'd won by a nose but was keen for some reassurance. Carol ignored him, instead rubbing Brian's loin to calm him, his golden coat was soft and fleece like to touch. She noticed that Brian was wearing a name tag on his collar, on the back was an engraved phone number. She reached for her phone and dialled. As she placed the phone to her ear, she could hear distant music. Relief. Brian's owner was clearly on route to the summit, he wasn't a handsome stray.

A few seconds later, Brian's mum appeared, jogging at an impressive rate given the gradient and tough terrain. She stopped her watch timer the second she reached the toposcope. *Perhaps in hope of a personal best?* Carol wondered. She looked a serious runner, and an impressive athlete. Wearing a woolly orange hat, orange sunglasses, grey figure-hugging base layers and orange trail trainers, there was a professional look to her. Carol guessed she was maybe 20 years her junior. As she walked towards Carol, it was clear this was a stunning looking woman: no make up, a gleaming smile, her natural blonde hair in perfect pigtails. She had an athletic build, toned, yet curvaceous.

"Apologies about Brian, he can get a little boisterous on trail runs, I hope he didn't disturb you?"

"Not at all," replied a bubbly Carol, "I was just rehearsing a speech for a friend's wedding, I don't normally see anyone up here at this time."

"Thought I'd take advantage of the beautifully fresh weather. My partner's away on business so I can actually work off my own diary for once," joked Brian's mum.

"Fancy a coffee?" Asked Carol in a friendly voice.

"Aw, that would be lovely, you get cold quick up here."

"Listen, if you need a wee proofreader I'd be happy to help. Ever thought of doing a poem for them?"

"A poem? That's a lovely idea. Thanks so much-"

"Oh, how rude of me," stated Brian's mum. My name is Amber, very pleased to meet you. The captivating eye contact, the warm smile, the gentle handshake. In that moment, Amber seemed so genuine.

The pair would go on to meet up every second Sunday; running, chatting, drinking coffee. Life just couldn't get any better for Jeff and Brian, a full morning with their favourite human and their doggo bestie. As trust developed over time, Carol disclosed a number of personal issues, as did Amber. Carol knew hers to be true but was now questioning the authenticity of every single statement that passed Amber's lips.

As she sat on her sofa, Carol took a final sip of her coffee and started to think about past conversations. She remembered talking about fertility issues from several years back. It became a huge challenge for her and Martin, and no doubt placed significant pressure on their marriage at that time. Sarah was eventually conceived through IVF. Carol was 37 when she was born. Amber had always stated that Jim was mad keen on having a family but she remained unsure because of her own childhood experiences. Of course, she then had Lucas so something clearly changed her mind along the way.

Carol also recalled discussing mental health episodes. Martin suffered a crisis having been promoted at school. He struggled for months, maybe years to separate and balance the pressures of work and life. Amber revealed that she'd battled with drug and alcohol addiction, so had Jim. Running and painting had helped to save her.

Carol then obsessed over Amber's relationship with Jim. So many times Carol had invited them over for a Sunday lunch or a Friday night dinner party. When Rachel was alive and well she'd tried to get the trio together for shopping trips. Amber constantly had an excuse. They often had plans with family. Jim seemed to have endless business commitments. Carol questioned her own criticality, *was Jim even a real person? Or was he a made up character, created by the warped mind of Amber?* Amber spoke about James, far more than she'd ever speak about Jim. With hindsight, nothing felt right.

Carol was drawn back to her downstairs cupboard. She picked up her diary from 2019 and returned to her sofa, the snoozing Jeff hadn't moved an inch.

Again, Carol's diary entry painted the clearest of pictures. Sunday, 12th May 2019. Carol, Amber, Jeff and Brian jogged up Arthur's seat to watch the sunrise over the city. Once more she tried to recall the exact conversation. Amber had asked about her plans for the week ahead. "Busy one at work and then I'm babysitting James' baby boy Charlie. He's been through hell as you know. Martin has agreed to take him to the football, then likely a few drinks up town."

"Oh that's lovely, Martin is such a sweetie," replied Amber.

"He sure is. The problem with Martin though, when he goes out, he goes out out. They'll no doubt end up dad dancing at a CC Blooms or somewhere until 2:30am.

"Haha, boys will be boys eh." A jovial smile from Amber.

With hindsight, the seemingly innocent chat appeared to be the final piece of a deceptive jigsaw. Carol placed a hand on Jeff for comfort and security. When she consciously listed Amber actions, they chilled her skin...

- She'd co-created James and Rachel's wedding poem.
- She'd helped Carol to grieve after the passing of Rachel.
- She'd lied about her profession, possibly her partner.
- She'd facilitated a friendship between Charlie and Lucas.
- She'd regularly sited the handsome good looks of 'stranger' James.
- She'd expertly positioned herself at that bar back in 2019.

But, to what end? It was clear, nothing was by chance. Everything had been well thought out. Amber had in some part been directing James' life from a far, manipulating Carol and others along the way. She wanted to call her out for her deceit, and would in due course, but James was the clear target, not her. It was important he got answers, some kind of closure, some kind of justice. He was due to call Amber that day.

CHAPTER 25

WE ARE ALL GUILTY

Monday, 4th December 2023.

Playful growls and uncontrollable laughter echoed through an expansive ground floor. Teddybear tug of war was in full swing. Brian and Lucas would play fight all day if they could. Very often their mum would intervene before things got too rowdy though. But, not on this occasion. A preoccupied Amber sat at her kitchen table, staring intently at her call list, a notepad and pen lay to her right. She'd 'missed' four calls from James the day before, each one accompanied by a desperate voicemail. For years she'd longed for him to make contact, but not now, not like this. She knew a shitstorm was coming her way.

After the fourth call, she replied by text. "James I can't talk right now. Can we speak face to face? I'll come to your house. Tomorrow afternoon?" A one word reply from James, "Yes." She scribbled down awkward discussion points, possible challenge questions, likely responses and best/worst case outcomes. She thought carefully about her voice tone and variance, her presentation and body language. She needed to come across as lonely and confused, not psychotic and sadistic.

Amber had a big day ahead of her. An early morning phone call from the prison invited her to meet with Frank at 11:00am, an unusual visit time. She text James as soon as she'd hung up, "Be at yours for 1:00pm." Another succinct reply, "Okay."

A bubbly Gayle arrived to babysit Lucas, she loved nothing more than spending time with her grandson, he'd given her a new lease of life. "Thanks so much mum, the two of them have been pretty hyper all morning. Feel free to give Lucas some IPad time before lunch." Gayle nodded her head. "This feels like a big moment Amber, why do you think they've asked you to come in?" Amber shrugged her shoulders, "I've no idea mum. Now that he's full committed, maybe a change of prison? Or maybe a confirmed date for the High Court? Time will tell I guess." Amber paused. "Oh, I've got a couple of things to do after I've spoke with Frank. I might be out for a wee while, that okay?"

"Course it is darling. Take your time. After lunch I'll take the boys to the park. Lucas can play on the swings and I'll throw Brian's ball a thousand times!"

"Haha! They'll love you for that."

"Oh Amber, whilst I remember, you still wanting me to take Brian for a couple of nights yeah?"

"Yes please mum, that would be amazing." Amber grabbed her car keys and handbag. "One more thing before I go mum. Can you please give me a call at 1:15pm?"

"Yeah, course I can, everything okay?"

"Yeah all good thanks." Amber hugged Lucas and thanked her mother for a final time. She walked outside, filled her lungs with a deep breath, then got into her car.

Amber entered the visiting hall at Saughton Prison. A lean looking Frank sat by himself towards the back of the room, his head was bowed. He began speaking the second Amber sat down. His speech was monotone and slow. "I don't want this being a drawn out affair Amber, I'll just cut to the chase, alright?" Amber felt immediately uneasy. "Eh, yeah, okay Frank."

"I'm changing my plea to guilty." The announcement took Amber's breath away, she was in disbelief. "What?! No. Frank no. You can't do that." Frank attempted to comfort her, holding both her hands in his. He raised his head and engaged in eye contact. His pitch remained the same. "I can, and I will. Don't be upset. It's the right thing." Amber responded through tears, "The right thing for who? Lucas needs his dad, Frank." Frank sighed, "Lucas will be just fine Amber. I'll make sure of that. This has to happen. Craig and I have discussed the process and outcome at length. I'm fucked, I've made too many mistakes. The police have got everything they need and more. If this goes to court, it'll be a media circus. You'll be dragged into it, as will Rambo, and Joseph, and Steph, and your mum, and anyone else connected with the family. Amber replied, "But Frank, you're a fighter, you're never beat."

"What I am Amber is a very bad man, who's done terrible things over many years. It's time I paid for my crimes. This way, Lucas gets to live a normal life and our fucked up little secret never sees the light of day. Me shooting James was mistaken identify, I shot the wrong guy. I'm guilty. That's our story, end of."

"So what happens now?" Queried a sniffling Amber.

"The plea will be entered and then I'll be sentenced. Attempted murder carries the same weight as murder. Craig reckons pleading guilty so early might help me in someway, but fuck knows." Amber responded again, doubling down. "Frank no, I can't accept this, I won't. You could be looking at 20 years. This needs to go to court, there's always a chance, you've got the best lawyer money can buy. There could be a problem with evidence, a technicality, anything.

Frank groaned in frustration, raising his voice, he stated, "Let me spell it out Amber so it's very fucking obvious. You think I'm going to shame myself in front of a judge and jury? I'm Frank Smith, I run this fucking city. My Mrs has been raped, my son is a bastard, my succession, my legacy is fucked. You expect me to sit and listen to you and daft Rambo giving evidence in court? Fucking no chance. And no fucking way am I giving that whore Taylor the opportunity to publicly laugh in my face. No, I'll take the hit, like a proper fucking bossman."

The couple embraced in a prolonged hug, Amber gripped on for dear life. "I love you Frank." Frank didn't respond. He remained stoic as he was led away by two guards. Amber slowly made her way to the exit door, but a sudden shout stopped her in her tracks. Frank announced, "Sorry Amber, I meant to say. I never ever got round to wiring up that bloody doorbell. Get Stevie the electrician to connect it for you. That way I know you and Lucas are safe." Amber nodded, "Eh, yeah. Sure Frank."

Amber sobbed as she walked out the exit door and through the car park. But, as she approached her own car, everything changed. Tears were replaced by a smile, then a laugh, then an uncontrollable cackle. She felt like a real life Harley Quinn escaping Arkham Asylum. For maybe the first time in her life, Steph was wrong. The streetwise Frank could indeed be framed. Framed by the insecure, capricious and chaotic Amber. She had finally out witted 'The Cunt's Cunt.' She was officially free, what a fucking buzz. Once seated, she attempted to reapply her make-up in the drivers rear-view mirror. It took several minutes, her hands shivered with adrenaline.

Once happy with her look, she drove to a nearby coffee shop to reset her nerves and read over her notes. Amber thought to herself, The *Frank nightmare is over, Lucas and I are safe. But, James fucking hates me.* She'd have to live with that.

Amber parked outside *James*' house at 1:02pm. Her conversation with Frank was a cakewalk compared to this one. In her mind it was Frank who'd forced her into the dark world of corruption and deceit. She was far from innocent, but did what she had to do to survive. She knew James could never find out about her relationship with Frank, it would totally fuck her escape plan. She thought to herself, *Frank deserves everything that's coming his way. James on the other hand, is just the unfortunate victim in this bizarre narrative. She never intended for him to get hurt.* She practiced positive affirmations before approaching the front door of number 39. "You're a great person, stay calm, stay strong, you've won." She knew the painful conversation would be short. A fabricated childcare phone call was about to bail her out in thirteen minutes.

CHAPTER 26

FROZEN IN TIME

Monday, 20th May 2019.

Amber returned home after dropping James at Bramble Place. She'd nipped to her mother's house on route to pick up Brian. Once she'd given him his breakfast kibble, Amber raced upstairs to her bedroom and began stripping the fluid stained sheets and pillow cases. She opened several windows and began a full clean of the house.

After hoovering everywhere, she mopped all solid floors, ironed and fitted new bedding, and sprayed perfume throughout the upstairs. She then nipped outside to the garage, sliding the cracked wall mirror underneath a steel storage shelf. After four or five shuttle runs she'd returned a dozen picture frames and a single vacuum flask to the house. The picture frames were all personal photographs of Amber and Frank, including a huge canvas portrait of the couple. She rehung it at the base of the staircase and repositioned the others on window sills, worktops, tables and sideboards. Previously taken photographs from her camera roll reminded her of exact locations and tilted angles, if anything was out of kilter, Frank would notice it.

She reordered the large mirror from Amazon, luckily an exact match was available and would arrive the next morning. Before tossing her dirty bedding into the washing machine, Amber pressed James' sweaty pillow case against her face, inhaling his scent like a well-trained sniffer dog. She smiled fondly as she shut the door and selected the hottest wash cycle possible. A cover up Rambo would be proud of.

Amber was back in her car at 12:15pm. A deluge of rain increased her journey time to nearly three hours. But, neither the weather or distance troubled her. As far as Amber was concerned, this was step one towards salvation. A few miles in, she decided to stop off at Queensferry to get herself a large latte and croissant, hoping that caffeine and sugar would cure her tiredness. Almost all of the journey was a day dream of future wishes and aspirations. She found herself fast-forwarding five years, 17 years, and 21 years into the future. She smiled with excitement and enthusiasm. Yet, as she parked up at her destination, a seed of doubt entered her mind. *Had she gone too far? Was this response just too extreme?*

Amber stared at the entrance door and company signage from the comfort of her cabin. She used the sun visor to part hide her face. Seven long minutes passed as she waited for the final member of reception staff to leave. She'd been clearly instructed, "Arrive no earlier than 3:20pm."

What Amber was about to do was radical, no doubt, but the actions of Frank had driven her into a corner she couldn't escape from. This was the only way she could move forward with her own life, hopefully creating some sort of loving connection as part of the process. She reminded herself, *you have to do this Amber.* The teeming rain subsided for a brief moment. She exited the Range Rover and put up her umbrella, before grabbing a navy blue rucksack from the back seat. She hopped and skipped over deep puddles before entering the STF Fertility Clinic in Aberdeen.

Amber turned a set of keys, securing the main entrance. She then walked towards a second door at the end of the brilliant white reception area. She took a deep breath as she turned the handle and entered the clinic room, closing the door behind her.

"Did anyone see you?" Asked a confident female voice.

"No, no one. I did as you said, everyone is gone, and the front door is locked."

"Good girl." Steph logged off her computer, spun around and rose from her chair, embracing her best friend with a warm hug.

"Right, you got it yeah?"

"Yeah I've got it." Amber opened her rucksack and passed over a small vacuum flask.

"The fact that you're standing and breathing in front of me, I'm guessing you've kept this hidden from Frank?" Asked Steph.

"Eh, yes, it's been well stashed in the garage for the last two months. It took forever to get things planned and set up properly. I only knew I was definitely going through with it on Friday night. James eventually agreed to go out with Carol's man Martin."

"And the flask has been sealed the whole time yeah?" Asked Steph.

"Yes, other than transferring the semen, it has never been opened."

"Great, and the timeframe from ejaculation to storage?"

Amber giggled. "Gees, I don't know. Maybe seven, eight minutes."

"Good, so some cooling time before it hit the nitrogen. And the pipette?"

"Disposed of. It's in a park bin in Queensferry. There's no chance of Frank suspecting anything."

"Just as well Amber. You know the dangers for me, this can never get out, ever. This remains between you and me until we're in the ground, agreed?"

"Agreed. Steph, you are saving my life here. I'll never forget what you're doing for me."

Steph slipped on a pair of cryogenic gloves and opened the flask, causing a cloudy vapour to cascade down its outer shell. With her right hand she pulled the central console to the neck of the flask, using surgical tweezers in her left hand, she lifted out one of six plastic cylinders. Steph referred to each of them as straws.

"Seven straws, excellent, that should give us multiple opportunities to get this right, provided the semen has survived and is of good quality."

"Semen quality?! You gynaes crack me up! Man am I glad I dropped out of medical school!"

"How many times have I told you? I'm an embryologist!" Both women chuckled, as Amber sat on the examination bed.

Steph took Amber through the complicated IVF cycle stage by stage. "First things first, many couples are unsuccessful, I need to be clear on that. However, James has obviously fathered a child before, which is good news for us. Our biggest challenge could well be the length of time you've been on the contraceptive pill." Amber replied, "Yeah, I hear you. I've been on it since uni, but stopped taking it maybe four months back. Frank thinks I've been au naturale for the past two years!" Steph shook her head, "fucking hell."

"Hey you! No cold feet, you promised!" Pleaded Amber.

"Don't worry missy, I've got you. We just lead very different lives, that's all." Amber bit back, "well, as of this minute we're living the same fucking life, and I need your input to survive." After a brief stare off, Steph gave a reassuring smile.

"So Amber, stage one of the cycle involves a process called ovarian stimulation, this typically takes 12-14 days and involves you taking fertility hormones from the first day of your next period. When is that?"

"I'm due in eight days."

"Good. Stage two of the cycle is what we call egg retrieval. I will collect your eggs and essentially mix them with James' sperm in the lab. So you'll need to have a good excuse to be in Aberdeen that day. If his sperm count is low, or, if they are lazy swimmers I might have to consider a intracytoplasmic sperm injection, or ICSI for short."

"And that is?" Inquired Amber. "ICSI means that I manually inject your egg with a single sperm. That's obviously more complicated and carries a far higher fail rate. Stage three is fertilisation. This typically takes between two and six days. I'll then select the strongest developed embryo to be transferred back into your womb, and that's stage four. The fifth and final stage is the dreaded pregnancy test, which is taken 16 days after a successful egg retrieval. So yeah, a lengthy process, an intricate process."

"Steph you said many couples are unsuccessful. What we talking?"

"The chance of a successful outcome in cycle one is typically around 25%. However, that number jumps to 65% after five or more cycles. Of course the problem is, most patients give up long before cycle five due to the emotional and financial strain that comes with multiple failed IVF attempts."

"Five or more? Fucking hell."

"As I said Amber, you're a special case. We know James to be fertile, and we have no reason to believe you aren't. But you need to be patient with the process and diligent with your preparations. That means no drink, no drugs, good sleeping patterns, balanced diet. And, keep that fucking pig Frank away from you."

"Don't you worry, I'm on my A game for this, there will be no fuck ups. And to be honest with you, a longer time frame keeps James safe. Frank knows I was out last night, he's not back from Amsterdam until tomorrow evening. Say it takes a few cycles to work, I just need to sleep with him a couple of times after a positive test, then it's a case of 'congratulations Franky boy!'"

"It all seems so simple and normal when you put it like that Amber."

Amber returned to Aberdeen on several occasions for confidential IVF treatments. She was relentless in her pursuit of pregnancy and motherhood. After four months of disappointment and setbacks, she read her first positive pregnancy test on Friday, 27th September 2019.

CHAPTER 27

A FATHER'S LOVE

Tuesday, 5th December 2023.

James was so angry with himself. He'd failed to coax any meaningful explanation out of Amber. She'd played him for a fool all over again. He thought to himself, *Why in gods name did I agree to 24 hours think time?* He eventually decided to call Carol and relayed the bizarre conversation.

"She's sharp as a tack James, we both know that. I can't believe you waited a full day to tell me this. I need to confront her as soon as possible. In fact, I'm just gonna rock up at her door. So long as my 4:30pm meeting doesn't overrun, I could be there for 6:15pm. She won't be expecting a visitor, hopefully I can catch her cold and get some proper bloody answers."

Amber's watch ticked passed 6:00pm. Lucas sat heavy-eyed in his car seat. The cabin felt horribly stuffy, hot air belted the heavily frosted windscreen. Amber turned on the radio and selected Forth One to keep him settled. Little did Lucas know, in two hours time he'd be on an plane to Marseille. A night flight made a lot of sense, Amber hoped Lucas would sleep on board, keeping him fresh for a lengthy French road trip in the morning. In less than 24 hours they'd be in peaceful Provence. Amber envisaged herself sipping a glass of rosé beside a log fire, a subtle lavender perfume scenting the country air. She smiled with contentment as she packed the last of their bags into the boot. After hearing that Frank had pleaded guilty, Olivia offered to host Amber and Lucas. Olivia's family had a number of vineyard cottages available in the off season. Nothing permanent of course, but as long as she needed to finalise plans for her and her boy.

Amber had a final check for her mobile, sunglasses, passports, euros and credit cards. "Shit!" She spouted. "Where did I put my bloody phone?" She turned to Lucas, "Silly mummy. I won't be a moment darling." She kept the drivers door open to assure Lucas she'd be right back. The engine ticked over, the music continued to play. Lucas remained docile and relaxed in the back seat.

Amber re-entered the house, she remembered leaving her phone on the far side of the kitchen table. She'd lifted and carried a tired Lucas to the car just minutes before. She returned to the exact assumed spot, but, no phone. She scanned all worktops and checked under the table itself, just in case Lucas had knocked it or picked and thrown it - common behaviour from the toddler. Still nothing. Neither her or Frank ever wanted a house phone so she had no way of dialling her number. Amber's time was precious, she had to get to the airport, take off was in two hours. She needed her phone for flight information and boarding passes. *Ah! Find my iPhone*, she thought. She selected 'find device' on her Apple Watch, and, sure enough, the device began to ring. Strangely the noise came from the living room, she hadn't been in there since lunchtime. With Frank permanently behind bars, Amber's anxiety levels had reduced significantly. For maybe the first time ever she was comfortable and confident in her own home. She simply assumed that the innocent Lucas had inadvertently hidden her phone.

Amber nonchalantly entered the darkened room and flicked the light switch on. Almost instantly, she froze, her eyes strained, her mouth open. After maybe three seconds of shock induced stiffness, she inquired nervously, "R-r-r-ambo, what are you doing here?" The question was accompanied by a forced, panicked smile. Rambo stood in the centre of the living room, dressed in all black, his face shadowed by a dark hoodie. He held Amber's phone in his left hand, his index finger halting the ringtone. Amber quickly scanned his body, his right hand was tucked in his jacket pocket. Her eyes filled with tears. A feeling of pure dread overwhelmed her. A mumbled beg followed, "Rambo, please, I can explain-"

"Enough Amber, you've spoke enough. It's time to listen." An emotionless Rambo highlighted Amber's transgressions. "That Thursday night, you asked me to move Frank's jeep." Amber replied, she couldn't bring herself to act, but knew she'd have to repeat her fictitious words, "I needed into the garage."

"Ah, the garage." Responded a sarcastic Rambo. "The fucking garage! Clever little bitch aren't you? Asking me to reverse away from the front door, and the Ring doorbell. So you could slip Frank's coat underneath the boot floor, just before he left to meet Joseph."

Frank's doorbell comment from the day before slapped Amber across the face. She tried to speak but was immediately cut off. "And imagine forgetting to tidy up after yourself."

"What do you mean?" Queried a now sobbing Amber.

"The loose condom in Frank's glove compartment. Tut-tut, you naughty girl. What happened? Too pissed to remember? Out your tits on gear?"

"Rambo please-"

"I'm not done. You see, you made a one final, fatal error Amber. Just the other day, Frank shared his banking details with me. I did a wee check on the gallery credit card. 25th October 7:55pm, somebody spent £18.99 in Currys, Craigleith Retail Park. What's the only item in the shop marked at that price? A SIM Free Nokia 105." Rambo afforded himself a little smile. "I've got to hand it to you Barbie. It was almost a fucking masterplan. But, now me and you have a problem. Don't we?"

Just for a second, Amber thought about trying to turn and run. But, truthfully she knew she couldn't escape. As she feared, in

Rambo's right hand, a 9mm automatic pistol with an attached silencer. He raised his arm, the cold movement was accompanied by deafening silence. He stared into her broken, pleading eyes. The pause seemed endless. All Amber could think about was Lucas. A desperate tearful whisper, "Rambo, I'm a mother, don't do this."

"Sorry, but, he did say you'd be taken care of." A gentle press of the trigger, a single bullet to the heart. Rambo's kill count was in the tens, he was pinpoint accurate, 100% reliable. Amber fell backwards, her eyes wide but lifeless. She lay on her back, gasping for her final intake of oxygen. Blood poured from the wound, staining the ivory rug. Rambo hauntingly stood over her; a living, breathing Grim Reaper. A second clinical chest shot confirmed death. Typically, Rambo would normally shoot between the eyes but felt it was poetic to preserve her beauty. He exited the living room, and then the house via the back door, returning the building to darkness.

Moments later Carol's Ford Kuga pulled up beside Amber's Mini Cooper. The engine was still running, music continued to play, the drivers door was open, as was the boot. Carol quickly scanned the back seats, nothing. She approached the front door of the house, noticing immediately that it was ajar. She pushed it open and entered.

James and Charlie laughed and joked as they decorated their Christmas tree in the living room. They'd almost devoured a full box of Celebrations, only nine Bounty's survived the onslaught. "Right kiddo, lets count down! It's time to light this baby up!" Charlie counted down, "5-4-3-2-" A ding-dong halted the big reveal. "Was that the door Charlie?" There was an apprehensive tone to James' question. Charlie nodded his head. Since that night with Frank, any knock or chime sent both into a heightened state of panic. As always, James wanted to appear in control. "You eh, you stay here pal, I'll get it." James tiptoed along the hall towards the front door, hoping whoever pressed the doorbell had fucked off by the time he answered. He slowly opened the door, just enough to see out. No one. He scanned right, then left. No one. He thought to himself, *The kids of Morningside playing Chappie? World's gone mad.* Just before he shut the door, James glanced downwards. "Oh for fuck sake," he muttered.

A designer holdall lay on the black and white tiles. *What the fuck is this?* He thought. James' brain flooded with intrusive questions. A nail bomb? A letter bomb? Anthrax? Novichok? He scanned the darkened street again, no one. He bent down to cautiously unzip the bag. As he did, he heard imposing foot steps approaching. He looked up in slow motion, fear yet again engulfed him. For the second time in six weeks, he was about to be confronted by a blackened stranger on his own doorstep. But, what happened next brought confusion, not terror.

A monster of a man handed Lucas over to James, placing him gently into his arms. James couldn't move, he wanted to, but he couldn't. "Frank says sorry. There's plenty of clothes in the bag and I've included all his bank details. You now have full access to his accounts. Funds will be transferred every month, it will appear as M Rankin." James opened his mouth to speak but no words came out.

The man left as quickly as he'd arrived. A shattered Lucas cuddled in tightly. James' shocked brain eventually directed his body to reach down and pick up the bag. He turned numbly and walked into the vestibule, kicking the front door shut with his left heel. He slowly wandered back along the hall then gently lowered Lucas onto the living room rug. Charlie ran over, bursting with excitement. The two brothers began to play. Suddenly Lucas was full of energy again. James simply sat on the sofa in a trance like state, he stared at the pair and eventually smiled.

Rambo returned to the pickup. He put on his seat belt and turned on the engine. Just before pulling away, he glanced towards his passenger and winked. "Hey, Jamie boy, when we get back to mine I need to give this thing a wee clean. How about we get a chippy on the way home?" Jamie smiled, "Sounds class uncle John. Is it okay if I put some music on?"

"Course it is," replied Rambo. Jamie searched for his favourite song then pressed play, Rambo reached over and turned up the volume. The Man Comes Around pulsed through the speaker system. Rambo braked gently as he reached the end of Bramble Place. He indicated left and turned onto Morningside Road. As the song stated, Rambo was now the man taking names. As judge, jury and executioner, he decided who to free and who to blame. A new era was about to begin.

■■

ABOUT THE AUTHOR

John Duncan Millar was born 18th June 1987. He has enjoyed a varied and successful career as a farmer, teacher, app developer, textbook writer, football player and coach. His passion for learning, and his continued drive to try new things tempted him into the world of fictional writing in 2023. John lives in central Scotland with his wife Caroline, son Andrew and cockapoo Roxy. The couple look forward to welcoming another baby boy into the world in January 2025.

Printed in Great Britain
by Amazon